Nuala Ní Chonchúir

THE WIND ACROSS THE GRASS

ARLEN
HOUSE

The Wind Across the Grass

is published in 2009 by
ARLEN HOUSE
(an imprint of Arlen Publications Ltd)
PO Box 222
Galway
Ireland
Phone/Fax: 353 86 8207617
Email: arlenhouse@gmail.com
www.arlenhouse.ie

ISBN 978–1–903631–36–2, paperback
ISBN 978–1–903631–46–7, hardback

International Distribution:
SYRACUSE UNIVERSITY PRESS
621 Skytop Road, Suite 110
Syracuse, New York
USA 13244–5290
Phone: 315–443–5534/Fax: 315–443–5545
Email: supress@syr.edu
www.syracuseuniversitypress.syr.edu

Typesetting by Arlen House
Printing by Betaprint
Cover Artwork by Pat Jourdan
Gráinne Meets Queen Elizabeth, 1593

THE WIND ACROSS THE GRASS

Drumcondra Branch'

CONTENTS

ACKNOWLEDGEMENTS

'The Queen of All Ireland' was first published in *The Stinging Fly*.

'Island Woman' was first published in 'New Irish Writing' in *The Sunday Tribune* and was nominated for the Hennessy Award.

'Bone, Flesh, Marrow' was first published in 'New Irish Writing' in *The Sunday Tribune* and was nominated for the Hennessy Award.

'Watching the River' won the Cathal Buí short story prize.

'A Seatown Affair' was first published in *west 47*.

'The River Flows On' won the Cecil Day Lewis Award, was first published in *west 47* and *The Cúirt Annual 2004* and won the inaugural Cúirt New Writer Prize in 2004.

'Pig Alley' was shortlisted for the FISH Short Story Prize.

'Kicking Up Murder' was first published in *Whispers and Shouts*.

'Any Man's Fancy' was first published in *Northwords* (Scotland).

'Fleece' was first published in *Ink* (England).

'Finger' was first published in *ROPES*.

'The See Saw' was published on *deaddrunkdublin* and illustrated by Shelby Watkins for the story art exhibition at the 2008 International Conference on the Short Story in Cork.

'The Wind Across the Grass' won the Francis MacManus Award, was broadcast on RTÉ Radio 1 and published in *Whispers and Shouts*.

'I, Paula' was shortlisted for the FISH Short Histories Prize.

'Ms De'Ath' was published in *Litro* (UK).

i.m. of

NESSA

sister, friend, guide

THE QUEEN OF ALL IRELAND

Babby had a turn in her eye, a lazy eye. She had big soft lips and mangled hair. In the morning she drank three raw eggs knocked to a runny mixture in her chrome cocktail shaker – a birthday present from your uncle Dan. She'd throw the eggs back into her craw and then smile, showing the gluey yellow mess stuck to her teeth. Babby was mammy's sister and she was the Queen of All Ireland.

She was always known as Babby even though the name on her birth certificate was Bríd. Mammy said granny never called her anything but Babby from the day she was born, because when she realised she was a bit funny she didn't want to use up the lovely name she had picked, which was Angela. The priest said granny would have to pick something and then he said: 'We shall give her the moniker of Ireland's holiest woman, Saint Bríd of the plains of Kildare'. And Dan said 'Moniker Schmoniker!' because he was back from New York. Granny agreed to name her Bríd to keep the peace, but called her Babby all the time anyway. The first time mammy told you about that you said 'Who is Moniker?' and they all laughed.

Babby was a show off. Even though she was fifteen and had boobs and all, she drove a tricycle. It was a special big tricycle and she would drive up and down the street with all her sets of rosary beads slung around her neck singing *Hail Queen of Heaven.* Everyone would say 'Ah, look at her,

God love her', even though she sang crowy and slobbered. You could ride a two-wheeler and sing lovely, but no one ever said, ah, look at you.

You didn't want an auntie who had crossed eyes and was fat and who everyone stared at and who sat on you and punched you in the belly. *And* who drove a three-wheeler. You wanted a movie-style auntie, who was pretty like mammy, and who called you poppet and gave you her cast-offs. That's why everyone was thrilled when Dan brought home a girl. Daddy said 'You could hardly call her a girl', but mammy said 'Shut up you', and that kept him quiet.

Dan's new girlfriend was called Sarah-Mary and she had pink lips and a perfume smell and two holes in her cheeks that were called dimples. Babby put her big pokey fingers into Sarah-Mary's dimples, who was very polite and just laughed, but it was easy to see that she was a bit afraid. Then Babby got out her cocktail shaker, even though it was long past breakfast time, and granny said 'Put it away, Babby', but she wouldn't, and she shook the eggs extra hard for granny's benefit and for Sarah-Mary's. She had a big puss on her and she insisted on sitting beside Dan at the dinner table, even though he was entertaining his new girl and trying to impress.

Anyway, Dan was obviously doing something right because next thing you know him and Sarah-Mary are engaged and there's happiness all around. Except from Babby. When she heard she went into the parlour and broke Dan's crystal that he won at the golf, but he just said 'Ah, well' even though you hoped he would go mental and Babby would get in for trouble. She always got away with murder, you thought, and she was too big to be breaking someone's prized possessions on purpose.

You were thrilled about the wedding, never having been at one before, and then Sarah-Mary trebled your happiness by asking you to be her flower-girl. You were in heaven. But not for long, because Babby threw another fit when she realised she would just be an ordinary guest, whereas you would be the star of the show.

'I'm the Queen of All Ireland', she roared, and granny said 'Now, Babby, you're too big to be a flower-girl', and then Babby hit granny and there was wigs on the green all around. Then uncle Dan, the fecker, butted in and said 'Maybe Babby could be a flower-girl too', and your heart was filled with dismay like the girls in the comics. And you could tell that Sarah-Mary was feeling the same way because she gave Dan a look. But Babby was grinning and kissing Dan with her sloppy lips and he was laughing, all happy and carefree. Then Sarah-Mary dropped the bomb: 'We can't afford *two* flower-girls, Daniel', she said, very low.

Babby looked awful silly in her flower-girl's dress, but she thought that she looked gorgeous and she fecked the rose petals all over everyone on the way down the aisle, and then she had none left for outside the church. You all ended up throwing rice at the happy couple and picking bits of flowers out of each others' hair for the day. Everyone told Babby that she was a smasher, but it was obvious they were only saying that to be nice.

Sarah-Mary and uncle Dan looked like movie star lovers and she said to you 'A word in your ear', singling you out, and then she said that you could be the god-mother of their baby. You were glad to know they weren't so much in love that babies would only get in the way of the magic. Daddy said 'The only thing new at this wedding is the cake', and started making noises like a gun. Mammy told him to shut up, but he just laughed and then mammy laughed too and the two of them were in convulsions. You didn't feel like laughing because it should have been you in a lovely dress strewing petals and at least you'd have done it properly.

But someday you would be a god-mother and that was better than being a flower-girl, really. So Babby could keep her stupid dress and her big fake smile for the camera and you'd see who would be the real Queen of All Ireland in the end.

Island Woman

This island woman, unused to sharing her borders, misses the sea's comforting invasion. Surrounded by the earthy smells of dry land, she longs for the fishy oily stench of home. Listening for the screeking of gulls and the reedy thwack of ropes, her ears fill with the plain inland noises she has come to hate: rustling leaves, birdsong, car engines. And now, new sounds: the warm hum of a hospital ward, where curtains are rattled roughly on iron poles and the nurses shout into your face, revealing your secrets.

The wind howls differently on the mainland, where there is nothing to look at but grey walls. The people here don't know what wind is; the breezes that blow around and about are little more than draughts. They don't know the comfort to be found in a howling gale when the boats are tucked safely in the harbour; that in-between haven that's made of neither land nor sea.

Ghost villages stand all around the island. Wintering geese and grey seals make up most of the population since the island woman, and the rest, were removed to the mainland after a storm came and stole many of the island's men. Bog cotton blows in solitary drifts on peaty stretches of land and water gathers in still pools on pathways. In the island woman's house a postcard of New York is pinned to the wallpaper with a rusted thumb-tack, and the roof above the hearth has collapsed, throwing mossy slates and rubble into the fireplace.

The island woman closes her eyes and leans back into the pillows, a liver spotted hand rubbing at her forehead, waves of memories washing over her.

She is standing ankle deep in red dulse, stretching, her hand rubbing at the small of her back, which has become sore from bending over. She looks around and realises that the rest of the women have also stopped working. They are walking away from their creels, some of them into the lacy edges of the sea, and they are shielding their eyes from the harsh autumn sun.

She moves towards the shoreline with them, drawn by their slow gait. Straining against the sharp sunlight, she looks to where Inis Beg follows Pig Island out to sea. She sees a turbulence in the water, a rise and gush and a glisten of black. Again, a rise and gush. It's the fins and backs of many whales, heaving in and out of the waves. They are orca, near enough to the shore for their sheen to be recognisable, chasing the salmon to warmer waters. It is the first time she has ever seen them, and she follows them with her gaze until all she can make out is the dim line of foam left in their wake. The work is easy for the rest of that day.

The hospital ward is sterile; washed of the stench of sickness, it proclaims its own smell of steely, clinical warmth. The island woman hates it here: the static cling of the polyester nightdress, the brusque foolishness of the nurses, the false reverence shown to the doctors. None of them seem to enjoy their work and she resents their intimate knowledge of her decaying body. But she is co-operative, despite herself, because mostly she is afraid.

The consultant stops by her bed, flanked by a posse of younger doctors.

'How are you?' he asks, scanning her chart, not expecting an answer.

His red hair sits in curves over his high forehead, the bracelet strap of his watch rattles and slides over his wrist as he clicks a biro. He stands, pen poised, looking scrubbed and worn.

The island woman drags herself up in the bed, pulling at the nightdress that has knotted itself around her legs. Needles of pain stab at her gut, and she pauses for a moment, her white hair straggling around her face. She pulls at the green waffled bedspread with her fingers, picking fitfully at the thinning threads, her eyes raking over the doctor's sandy hair. Her mouth lolls open and she looks confused; she can't understand how things have come to this. She leans back in the bed, strained and tired, and closes her eyes; the lids are puckered and slack. She lifts back the years in her mind.

A red-haired boy stands in front of her. She is pulling seaweed from a basket and leaving it to dry on the stone wall, and she doesn't see him until he is almost on top of her. She jumps, her hand flying to her mouth, and then she laughs. He smiles at her, a slow easy smile. Seagulls are mewling overhead and there is a warming Gulf Stream breeze blowing around the bay.

'I'm looking for Jim Conneely', says the boy, one hand hanging at his side, the other holding a tightly wadded bundle.

'I'll get my mother to speak to you', says the girl, sliding past him to the house, aware suddenly of the dirt on her bare feet.

She likes the look of the boy, his light hair, his casual stance and solidity, but she cannot let him into her mind. She is going to marry Martin Crehan, because Crehan's fields back onto her father's land. He is older than she is –

a lumbering fool well past middle-age – and his slobbering shyness sickens her. But it has been decided.

When she had passed Crehan in the back field a couple of days before the red-headed boy arrived to help her father, he had reached out and touched her breast with his fat red fingers. She ran away from him, tripping over grassy clumps and stones as she made her way home, and she spoke to no one for the rest of that day. Her mother passed no remark.

The lights have been dimmed in the ward. The island woman wakes to the soft chatter of voices, a yellow glow glides across the floor from the office where the nurses have gathered. From all around the room comes the sound of sleep disturbed by sickness: light snoring, rasped coughs, low moans. She is feeling hot, vague, and uneasy, and her thoughts are drifting without form. She has lost control of her fate once again.

The red-headed boy is in love with her; he holds her hand and kisses her neck when no one is looking. He winks at her in the kitchen when he sits at the table waiting for his food, and she helps her mother with the dinner. He is a fair worker, but his heart is not given to fishing or farming. He promises to send for her when he gets to America.

'We'll be the finest couple in New York', he says, twirling her around on the sandy shore, out of sight of the house. She believes him.

But when he's leaving, she knows by him that his thoughts are already halfway across the Atlantic, and that she is being left behind. There is an awkwardness in the hug he gives her, and he reproaches her when he sees her tears.

'Don't cry, ah for God's sake, don't cry. We'll be together again soon', he says.

She nods and snivels, then wipes the snot and tears from her face with the back of her hand. They are sitting on the sand, facing out to sea, watching a soft fog crawl its way towards them over Inis Beg. He stands up, moves off and waves, his easy smile breaking across his face. She watches him head to the harbour where a small boat will take him to the mainland.

His postcard arrives on Shrove Tuesday, the morning of her wedding, three months to the day after he left.

Her husband, Martin, stands over her, ghoulish in the half-light; his clothes sopping wet and decorated with tiny barnacles. His skin is dewy, it bears the blue-white sheen of buttermilk, and his lips have lost their full redness. His mouth barely moves when he speaks and his voice emerges as a low gurgling sound.

'You never loved me', he intones.

'No', she replies.

'Were you glad when I was taken?'

'Yes', she says, 'sorry'.

He moves off, hovering at a slow pace toward the glowing light, and she watches his retreat without fear or feeling.

Out on the island, some scraggled sheep are sheltering behind the wall of the island woman's house. Their legs trip and topple under them as they are blown about in the wind, and they turn and scrabble on the uneven ground, bumping into each other. A low moan descends from the roof of the house, followed by a pitched screech that sends the sheep scurrying from their sheltered spot.

She is slipping away. Her head is thrown back on the pillow and circles of mauve ring her closed eyes; there is a wheezing rattle in her throat. Her small chest rises and falls, and the dark hollow in her neck can be seen inside the collar of the floral nightdress she wears. Her hands are lying on the faded green bedspread, the thumbs curled and hidden inside her fingers. A low moan fixes itself in her mind. It rises to a familiar wail, and she finds herself glad to hear the sound for herself at last. She lets herself be carried off over the waves to home, drowning in the screeching keen that resounds all over the island.

BONE, FLESH, MARROW

There's a blood and sinew smell, a reminder of the abattoir and its caved-in pig ribcages swinging in rows, the slick of guts clinging to everything; a white place blasted with the ooze of blood. Bowditch calls it their field of gore, his words as thick as tallow spurting from his mouth. Then the meat market, packed with innards and offal and bones, giving off that same stink that swallows him here. Gill's arse-bones are on fire from the clabbery floor under him and the blindfold is biting into his temples. He is collapsed against a wall and he is so sore that he can't really feel himself anymore. He can hear a clack-clack-clack behind the wind outside, but can't make out what's causing it.

They had told him to get out weeks before but he didn't go. Now they have him. He laughs and the crack of his smile sends a spill of blood from his lip. He curls his tongue to taste it, finds it's not salty enough, and so he licks the back of his hand.

Bowditch, the scrawny animal, he thinks, if I ever lay eyes on him again I'll cleave him in two, from snout to rump. His laugh is a snort this time. He pulls at the blindfold and it comes off in a stiff round, his blood hardened through it. Gill throws it to one side before lifting his eyelids to the darkness. He trails his hand along the wall and then sniffs his fingers. The wall is damp and rough, like the earth floor he's sprawled on. It must be some kind of shed or outhouse, he thinks. He's sure there has to be a door off to his right because he can feel a draught at his feet. Pulling himself up onto his knees he sways there for a few moments waiting for the blast through his body to ease. Cold and heat bleed through him. He cradles himself and rubs his hands along his forearms trying to tamp down the hairs. Gill slumps forward and his breath comes deep and slow. He throws up, covering his mouth with his hand and the eggy mess sticks to his fingers.

'Oh, Jesus', he moans. They are the first words he's heard in what might be days, but they seem to come from outside himself. He passes out, thumping head first onto the floor. When he comes around he heaves himself up before he can decide not to move at all. His foot crunches under him and a cold sweat gasps across his forehead. He lurches and falls onto his side, his hand landing between his legs. It's only then he realises that they've taken his clothes.

Gill waits for another few minutes and then he scrabbles around the floor, half crawling and half pulling himself along, trying to cover the whole room. He must know the shape of the place, what else is in here, so that he might somehow get out. He lies face down to rest and sucks in the fug of the cold floor. There is a throb belting up and down his legs and arms and he knows it's all worse than he realises yet. He digs his fingernails into the floor trying to stir the clay but it's stiff and packed and he hasn't the strength to move it.

It was Bowditch, he thinks, it had to have been him. No one else could make him talk the way he could, the scrawny bastard. No one else could lead you into a conversation the way he did, padding his meaning with jokes and throw-aside laughs. He was stupid not to have seen him for what he was. But he had been taken in, mistaking the man's banter for friendship.

Bowditch had appeared from the air, now that he really thought about it. He had arrived one morning with Leeson, the owner, wearing a grey overcoat and a tight beard. His handshake had reminded Gill of dried fish: firm and flaky. He came with his own set of knives cradled in a soft leather pouch; no one had ever seen anything like them, with their mottled yellow handles. Bowditch wouldn't let anyone touch them, but he would hold them up to be admired and hint that they had come from somewhere far away, Eastern Europe maybe, or Russia. He was masterful with a knife. He could split a pig from belly to arse before the animal even knew where he was and there was never a squeal. He had a fast hand.

He had been put to work beside Gill who had treated him with the suspicion always given to a new man. But Bowditch just worked and sang aloud to himself, he didn't look for conversation, and after a while Gill and the rest began to get used to him. He followed them to The Curfew one night and then every night after that. Soon he was one of them, as in with them as it was possible to be. They weren't close. Even when one of them died – like the old man Carey – he was never missed. In less than a week they had closed around the gap left by Carey as if he'd never been there. Bowditch soon began to talk as much as the rest, but he didn't reveal much of himself. Gill tries to remember now where he was from, where he lived, if he was married, if he had children; he finds he can't.

He sees a grey line of light near the floor on the other side of the room. The bulge of the cuts around his mouth are making a thick slabber fall from his lips. He lifts his hand to swipe it away and starts to drag himself across the floor. But when he gets to where he thinks the light is coming from, there's nothing. He reaches out with his fingers hoping to find the smooth wood or steel of a door. The blood-iron smell is worse now, he realises, and it's clouded over with something worse. An old smell, a flesh and marrow smell. He feels the judder in his guts and he throws up again. By the time he's finished retching he's choking on sour air and worn out.

He gropes around again and his hands fall on something rigid and cold. He pulls back and feels a pounding behind his eyes. He shivers and the shivering takes hold until his teeth are rattling so loud he can't think of anything else. He sucks his breath and rolls his tongue to try to stop his chittering teeth. He bangs his fist against the wall and his hand drops down. He fingers the hard mound lying in front of him, knowing that it can only be a corpse.

The clack-clack-clack he had heard earlier is louder now, a frenzy. It reminds him of the docklands, of boats; he thinks it might be the slap of ropes against flagpoles. He moves away from the body that is slung against the wall and tries to remember something of what went before.

They were in The Curfew. Leeson was buying drinks for everyone but as usual he didn't sit with them. He leaned against the bar and watched them while taking deep drags on his cigarette. Every so often one of them would raise their glass to him and say 'Mr Leeson' and he would nod and pull his hand across his chin. The last time Gill looked up Leeson was gone. Bowditch, who was sitting across from him, was telling some yarn in his creamy voice about a poisonous cousin of the potato – the mandrake root – and how he'd been forced to eat it by a Chinaman in London. Gill never knew whether to believe Bowditch's stories or not, they were always told with a swallowed sneer.

Most of the men were drunk by then or getting there. Gill noticed Bowditch nod to someone at his back and leave his chair. When he looked around there was no one there and when he looked back, Bowditch was gone. Gill left his own seat and went outside. He could see two people stooped under a lamp by the pier, one of them was Leeson, he couldn't be sure of the other. He decided to take a piss in the alley by the side of the bar and the steam was just beginning to rise between the straddle of his legs when someone grabbed his arms and slammed his face into the wall. He could feel a blade at his apple, nicking it gently.

'We know about you, Gill', the voice hissed in his hear. 'Watch yourself'.

Then he was kneed from behind and he fell to the ground, his face landing in his own wet. He put his hand to his throat and lay there for a while before pulling himself up and reeling towards home. When Ray let him into the flat he asked him what he expected from men who were only a step beyond the animals they slaughtered every day.

'What makes you think it was one of them?' Gill had argued.

Bowditch had cornered him in the freezer-room the next morning. He sauntered in, pushed the metal door shut and stood inches from Gill. Their breath made clouds in the air between them.

'You alright, mate?' said Bowditch.

Gill stared into the other man's eyes, let a low snort and kissed the air between them.

Bowditch laughed and thumped Gill on on the shoulder. 'Go on, you little shit', he said. His eyes were dead.

Gill can feel himself start to float, his mind skidding away into a swarming daze. He shakes his head to try to stay awake; he lifts his leg, finds it unbearably heavy. My foot must be broken, he thinks. He reaches towards it and its shape is all wrong; the skin feels like the puffed out fungus on a tree trunk. He slumps back against the wall and tries to control his breathing. Deep breaths, he thinks, but the more he tries to concentrate on his breathing the tighter his lungs become.

His head is crowded with images: clouds trailing across the sky like salmon scales; Ray laughing in a bar that's fuggy with smoke; water slooshing over the bow of a boat; men following them down a street, barking things at them, himself and Ray running fast to get away. He has heard all about the gangs that go around, cleaning up towns, getting rid of anyone that they don't see as a fit. He can picture them, vigilantes, a mob of baying do-gooders, cursing filth though their teeth.

Sweat starts to lick its way over his skin even though he's numb with the cold. A fuddle of despair settles itself around him and he slips into an uncomfortable doze. He dreams about Ray. He's lying beside him on the bed and Gill can see the slope of his spine, the shorn back of his head. He reaches out to touch his skin and turn him around so that he can see him properly. He calls Ray's name and pulls at his shoulder, but when he turns him over there is nothing where his face should be, nothing but a melt of skin. It's like something from a surrealist painting. A loud crash and Gill jerks awake, but when his eyes struggle open the room is still dark.

The smell surrounding him is like a stench from his childhood; the time a dead fox went to maggots at the end of the laneway. He remembers running down there behind the houses every day to inspect the heaving body, glad that the fox, an interloper into the city streets, was dead. He would prod at the animal's rotting body with his foot, inviting and hating its hot, liquid, night-time smell. Gill moves his back against the wall and feels the sickness in his guts charging then fading.

He starts to think about who it could be that's thrown on the floor in front of him; who the body belongs to. His thoughts spread. Strange how you become just a body when the life leaves you. Not a person anymore, just a bag of skin holding together some useless organs and a collection of bones. Gill doesn't believe in an afterlife. He never has. The idea of it attracts him, but he knows it's just a foolish hope that people hold onto. Ray's belief in the hereafter annoys him. It's one of the few things that they differ on entirely. Gill often goes on at him about humans being only a clump of cells that function well for a couple of years but soon die away. And that's how it should be, he thinks. Ray usually laughs and says that he'll pray for Gill's warped, unsavable soul.

'Leeson', he says out loud. The name slurs from his swollen mouth. He finds it hard to believe that the boss man could have been involved. He always seems so mild; a decent man. Gill laughs again, a dry painful snigger. The pounding in his ears and face gets worse and the air in the room closes in on his skin, muffling around his nose and mouth like cotton wool.

Ray will be worried now. It's not like Gill to go missing, not like him not to call. He wonders how long he has been here. Surely it can't be as long as it feels? For the first time he allows himself to think about what might come next. His face and shoulders tighten but he hasn't the energy to move. It's so cold he can feel right through to the heart of his bones. With his two hands he lifts his right leg to find a better position for his swollen foot. The packed clay floor is nearer than he has judged and his leg lands with a thunk that makes him cry out. He drops his chin to his chest and lets a sob shudder through his lips.

'Oh God, oh Jesus'. His words split his lip and his tongue feels thick with the taste of blood; the heat and the salt of it. The wind rages outside. Gill slumps against the wall, legs splayed, his useless head propped in his hands and he cries.

Watching the River

It was the day after Willy Kelly had mopped the kitchen floor with his wife's unwilling head that it happened. I wouldn't have known so soon about either event, only I had been helping myself to the sweet taste of my Ma's Fosfor Tonic, and it had spilt all down the front of my pale summer dress. Like a dark wine.

I ran from the house to where Ma was sitting in a deckchair on the street with the neighbourhood women. They sat there every late-summer afternoon, and followed the sun as it slipped behind the houses, moving their chairs to find the dying slivers of heat and light. They sat in a row, with their set hair and floral aprons, and talked about who-knows-what.

Well, that day I was a witness to the kind of thing they talked about. As I stood there with my guilty stain, I heard old Mrs Kelly tell them all that her son, buck-toothed Willy, had mopped the dirty floor with his wife's beautiful curls. Amid their tut-tutting, my Ma turned and saw me, and presumed I hadn't heard. I looked at her and burst into tears, all the while trying to wipe the medicine stain from my dress by rubbing bunches of the material together. She grabbed me by the arm and pulled me towards her with a practiced jerk.

'What in God's name were you at?' she demanded, while I sniffed and sniveled, resenting the other women's sniggers.

I glanced sideways at them, embarrassed and angry.

'Ah, don't be too hard on her', said old Mrs Kelly softly, her head cocked like a bird's as she winked at me.

It was then that my friend Mikey Dove ran up, snot-nosed and panting, with the news that the body of a woman had been pulled from the river Liffey, in the field below our houses.

'Jesus, Mary and Joseph', the women hummed, glancing, open gobbed, each to the other.

'Who? Who? Who was it?' squealed Mrs Hanley, blessing herself over and over, like a demented nun.

'I dunno ...' said Mikey slowly, worried now because the details he had weren't good enough.

My Ma hauled herself from her deck chair, rising to stand on varicosed legs. Being the only telephone owner on the street, she was determined to ring someone – anyone – to see who might be able to elaborate on Mikey's news.

Mikey and I slipped away in the direction of the river, hoping to catch a glimpse of the corpse; raging we hadn't been the ones to find it. We'd spent the whole summer scanning the banks of the river for dead men, from a clearing in the huge snowberry bush at the bottom of the field. We'd never dreamt that there might be a dead woman. Or that we'd miss our chance.

Young Mrs Kelly was leaving the riverbank, sallow-faced and wearing an unironed dress, when we arrived. Her blue eyes were red-rimmed and swollen. I glanced sideways at her lovely hair, and tried not to picture her being held upside down, her curls rank and stinking as an ancient mop.

'It was a nurse from the hospital; a young girl', she intoned.

We ran to the spot she had left, still hopeful of a sighting, or of some evidence that what we had heard was actually true. Young Mrs Kelly moved away from us, hugging her bare arms around her slight body for protection.

I hated Mikey, and loved him. He was my only friend. He loved to call me a sap. He made me feel sad and bad that I was only a girl. My Ma cut his hair, and all his brothers' hair, every few months. Earlier that summer I had made her cut my hair as short as Mikey's, in an attempt to look more boyish, to be more acceptable.

'Your dress is gammy', he said matter of factly as we tried to locate the exact spot where the nurse must have been found. I gave him a small shove and he turned and pushed me back. We pucked and elbowed each other as we continued through the scalded grass searching for signs of death.

My Ma, and the other women, had followed us slowly to the riverbank, to the rushy, weedy edge, where the swampy smell was overpowering. It was strange to see them there: they looked out of place in their sandals and skirts. We knew them only in kitchens and on deck chairs.

The evening sun had left the riverbank and the women stood back, murmuring and shaking their heads, while we poked among the reeds.

'Come back from there, you pair', Mrs Hanley called out to us, and we glanced at her, ignoring her lack of authority as a childless wife.

'Come on, kids', my Ma said, urging us to leave the morbid feelings that had engulfed the place.

I said I'd follow her home in a while. Mikey and I wandered across the field and entered the cool-walled ruin of the coach-house by lifting back the canopy of ivy that covered the doorway. The familiar mossy smell of damp earth filled my nose and I breathed deep on the cellar-like air. We had various treasures hidden in the gapped walls of the ruin. I pulled out a tin filled with stones, each of which we had painted with grasses soaked in elderberry juice. They were decorated with Stone Age pictures of people and dogs and horses. I sifted through them to find our favourite: the dead man floating in the water. I showed it to Mikey.

'Yeah', he said, 'cool'.

'It's the coolest', I replied.

Half of the time we spoke the language of American TV: *The Brady Bunch*, *The Partridge Family*. They were the kind of kids we could never really be, but we hoped one day that we might turn out like them. We wanted to be the sort of kids you really only found on telly; kids who were attractive, obedient, super-friendly and talented.

We took the Drowned Man Stone and solemnly, in an unspoken ritual, crossed the field together and threw it into the murky Liffey. It was an offering to the dead nurse and her family, an apology to them for thinking that the drowned person would have to be a man. We were sorry that by wishing for death, we'd somehow made her die. I told Mikey that Willy Kelly had cleaned the floor with young Mrs Kelly's head, and he called me a sap. He hissed it into my face.

I stayed in Mikey's house that night, the stone-built house on the river where you could watch the canoes float by in the day, and listen to the hush of the weir at night. We stayed up for hours, watching the water in the half-light; the swirl of branches and leaves caught on the edges of the far bank, going nowhere. We scared each other with stories of dead nurses who could climb slimed granite walls and stand over you in sleep. I stayed awake most of the night, listening to the river swallowing its secrets as it passed below the curtainless window.

In the morning the radio tagged a brief story to the end of the news – misnaming our town – about the woman's body taken from the river. We felt a little famous, while we moaned about the lack of real detail in the news report.

Later that day my Da found the nurse's watch, a small silver-chained timepiece, wedged into the slime of the riverbank. He brought it home and, when she came in from the shops, he told my Ma what he had come across. Mikey and I were eating bread and sugar at the kitchen table and we looked over at each other, our eyes locked.

'Can we see it, Da?' I asked, pleading in a quiet way.

'What do you want to see it for?' asked my Da.

'I don't know, I just want to hold it for a sec', I said.

My Da took the watch from where he had stored it in a tin on the dresser and dangled it on its delicate chain in front of my nose. I took it from him carefully and held it in my cupped hands. It was cloudy with the murk of the Liffey and I gently touched the tiny face, with its upside-down features, before handing it to Mikey.

'Cool', he said, drawing the word out over his tongue, as he swung the watch on its chain, watching the dank water inside slosh back and forth.

My Da brought the watch up the hill to the hospital to give to the matron, refusing our solemn offer to accompany him.

Mikey and I spent the rest of that summer scanning the riverbank from the shelter of the snowberry bush, our perspectives widened. Now we spent our time looking for drowned people, as opposed to drowned men.

ODALISQUE

The model is cold. Her plum-coloured nipples stand taut and a rash of goose-pimples spreads down her body like a shiver. She stands with her back to the draughty windows, too far from where a small stove glows. Outside, the air whooshes in ever-colder gusts and the sky turns peacock blue in the dusk. The alabaster sheen from a church is the only brightness to be seen through the high windowpanes.

The model's hair, relieved of its pins, hangs around her shoulders in auburn waves. Her cheeks are flushed despite the chill of the studio and the steely feeling in her bones. It is her first time to model. She is the only female in the room and she is naked. She can feel the boom in her chest and the attention of many pairs of eyes makes her awkward. She avoids the gaze of the artists as they work, and concentrates on holding her pose. She keeps her eyes fixed on a distant point on the wall. This is what her friend Genevieve has told her to do. This, and to think of ordinary things.

She is unaware that for the most part the artist sees not the body, but the form: the slope of a thigh, the curve of the hairline, the fall of a wrist. His concern is not with her, or for her, but with how he might reproduce the lines of her body on the page. The artist's desire is to give solidity to the only dimensions paper will allow. She is merely a study, an exercise, an expansion of a lesson in anatomy. The model's name is Victorine.

Amongst the art students is a young man called Édouard. Unknown to the model he is the reason she is here this evening. Édouard is acquainted with Genevieve, her friend; he has often chosen her from among the girls at the model's market in the place Pigalle. He likes her cutting nose and Scandinavian hair. Lately he has noticed Genevieve drinking wine in the Café Guerbois in the company of the pale red-head who stands before him now; her small body round and sturdy. He has pleaded with Genevieve to convince her friend to model at the studio he attends, in order that he might feast on her flesh. If only with his eyes.

Édouard is making slow progress today. His charcoaled hand lingers over the breast he has sketched, perfecting the shading in the arcs and curves, adding a smudged softness to the swollen flesh. He shades the areola and the nipple with such care that it's clear he craves a palette of paint, so that he might add colour. He lifts his eyes to study the high arch of the model's brows, the soft mound of her belly. He contemplates the milky smoothness of her skin for a long time, his close-set eyes widening.

The model is thinking of her father. She pictures him pouring milk from a pitcher into an earthenware crock that stands on a scrubbed kitchen table. She sees the coarse cloth of the coat he always wears; the pale mud dried onto his shoes. The milk he pours is warm and its cloudy fumes hang in the air. This hot, thick smell is the smell of her father. He covers the crock with a thin cloth, carries it outside and sits it carefully into a small handcart, along with many more jars of a similar size. She sees his pockmarked cheeks and the flap of skin that hangs from his chin. He lifts his hand to wave goodbye to his wife and only child before setting off to the cheesemakers, which is half a mile away.

His daughter drags up images: the age spots on his hands, the rheuminess in his eyes, the deliberate nature of his steps. This is how he was the last time she saw him alive.

A voice slices through her thoughts; there is a light touch on her arm. She jumps, unsure and unsteady for a moment; she pulls herself back to the present.

'You may rest for five minutes, Mademoiselle', the voice tells her, 'just five minutes'.

She is handed a cloak to cover herself with, and she shivers into its dank fustiness, gladly pulling the folds of fabric around her numbing body.

The students light cigarettes and pipes, and laugh with each other. They share their matches and news. Some of them leave the studio in search of something to eat and drink; some cheap bread and wine to fill their groaning bellies. The model curves her body into a small chair and watches the men move around from behind the curtain of hair that has fallen over her face. She doesn't understand their world and disbelieves Genevieve who tells her that some of them are actually decent.

'They are ordinary young men, Victorine. The same as any man you would meet in a café. Except that like us they are short of a few *sous*! Some of them really are nice, quite the gentlemen'.

'Well', says Victorine, 'they wear peculiar clothes'.

Her friend has been in Paris for some months now and is a favourite model at this studio. The girls' misled mothers think that their daughters work as domestic servants. That's what most of the young women from their hometown do. But some girls have found that there are other ways to make money.

Édouard walks over to the chair where the model has wrapped herself in the musty cloak. She sees him approach and turns her head away.

'It is cold, Mademoiselle', he ventures.

'Yes', she replies, at first not looking up at the slight, fair young man who has addressed her, and who is now hovering off to one side of her seat. She notices that his fingers are pulling at his short beard and that he frowns a little. Inside the cloak, the model runs her hands along her arms, trying to press down the hairs that are standing on end. She curls her toes and pulls her feet in under her buttocks, searching for warmth.

'May I offer to get you some coffee?' asks Édouard. 'Or a drop of wine, perhaps?'

Victorine curves her head around to look at him, surprised at this kindness. Although her lips are tight and violet-coloured with the cold, she parts them in a smile. Édouard smiles back, admiring her small uneven teeth.

They leave the studio together, her arm tucked under his elbow, his woollen scarf wound around her neck. They trip down the steps. Both of them are small, neatly made, though she is rounded rather than slim. They bend their heads close like two birds seeking shelter; their voices are low. They tumble though Montmartre's narrow streets, passing the old women who sit mending in doorways; even on this cold evening they sit and darn and call to one another in the half-light.

Édouard pulls her into a tiny alleyway between two houses. He leans his back against a blood-smelling iron gate, and wrapping himself around her, kisses her on the mouth with his wind-chilled lips. His beard scratches at her chin and her tongue is hot in his mouth; he feels an ache grapple at him and his kisses become fiercer. Her hands find their way inside his coat and she claws at his shirt until she finds the heat of his skin. Her fingers are cold, but she rubs and kneads the flesh of his back until the warmth returns.

'Stay in my *atelier* tonight', he murmurs into her mouth, as he pulls her closer onto him, 'will you stay with me, Victorine?'

'I will', whispers the model.

Édouard has a son. He will marry his son's mother. He has stories of the sea and of the mustard light of Italy. As Victorine reclines on the *chaise longue,* dressed only in the jewelry of a streetwalker, she listens to Édouard's tales. He stands feet-squared at the easel, mixing his palette of monochromes, and talking to her in his educated voice. She likes to listen to him; she learns from him.

'Someday, Victorine, you must travel to Venice. It is a magical place. Did you know that instead of streets they have waterways there? One travels by boat in Venice, past houses the colour of faded roses, topped with russet roofs. Everywhere is water and reflected light'. His hand moves across the canvas in small waves. The model fiddles with the fabric of the painted shawl spread underneath her and she leans further back into the pale cushions that prop her up.

'How will *I* go to Venice?' she enquires. 'An artist's model is badly paid, as you know, Édouard'.

Ignoring her remark, he continues: 'And when you go to Venice, you must dine on sea-scallops at the Caffe San Fantin. They cook the most wonderful seafood there. Indeed, they have over one hundred years of practice, maybe that's why they are so good at it'.

The model listens, soaking in the soft hum of the painter's voice, trying to imagine a city where the streets are washed with water, wondering if she will ever see it.

'You know, you remind me of Titian's *Venus*', Édouard continues absently, dabbing at the palette, contemplating where the brush needs to go next. She smiles. She is not familiar with Titian, though she visits the museums often and recently has begun to paint herself. Small paintings, portraits mostly, that she completes in the silence of her own room.

'Stop smiling, Victorine', Édouard scolds, 'I want that same boldness in your expression that you had for me yesterday'.

'I will try, Édouard', she says, adjusting the dusky pink blossom in her hair, and flexing her fingers as she settles back on one elbow, fixing her gaze to one of quiet assurance. 'Talk to me about painting', she says.

'What do you wish to know?' he asks, his rhythmic walk carrying him to where his paints are laid out on a side table. He turns to look at her.

'Well, why do you paint as you do?'

Édouard thinks for a moment, the turned up edges of his mouth suddenly flattened and serious.

'I suppose I like things to appear as they really are', he ventures. 'As they are here and now, in their natural state. Everything changes with time, Victorine. Beauty changes, for example, and I like to paint beauty as it exists today. *You* know what I mean!'

'Yes, Édouard, I do know what you mean'.

'That's it, now, stay as you are, hold it like that', he breathes. 'You are my latter day Venus', and he begins to paint rapidly, his eyes flicking from the canvas to his model.

'*Olympia*', sneers the man to his friend. They stand in front of the painting; all the while he is tapping a gold-topped cane on the Salon's polished floor. 'The man is insane'.

Victorine stares down at them, her bare skin luminous against the dark background, a velvet ribbon tied at her throat.

'What exactly is he trying to achieve?' gasps his companion.

Groups of people have gathered around the painting. They have come to be scandalised, having witnessed the furore raging in the newspapers about the coarse female nude now hanging in the Salon.

'He leaves one feeling like a voyeur, it is most uncomfortable', says the first man.

Her eyes invite them to study the length of her body, to step into the painting and share a caress. The maid hovering with the bouquet of flowers will soon leave the room; the black cat can stay.

'And look at the expression on her face! She is little more than a prostitute!' says his friend.

'This Manet is a libertine. The Salon has refused him before; I cannot understand why they should allow the exhibition of such indecency now'.

The man taps his cane on the floor again, looking all around him for agreement. The crowd murmur and gasp, titillated by the immorality of it all, feigning their outrage.

Victorine looks on, comfortably settled against the silk cushions, her hand toying with the edge of the fringed floral shawl; a cream coloured slipper dangling from her tiny foot. She is ready to receive the world.

Édouard is married. Disappointed. Settled. Respectability has settled like a fog around him, but it will be short lived. He is a passionate man, he will die young.

Victorine has lost herself in a bottle. Her pearly skin has mislaid its sheen, and her smiles no longer break easily. An infrequent artist's model, she has fulfilled Édouard's prophecy for her, and she plies her trade from a dismal room in Montmartre. When the choice is her own, she chooses girls as lovers. She paints their portraits and sells them to the absinthe drinkers who gather in the cafés on the Boulevard Clichy. Soon she will leave the hum of the city for the suburbs, and she will live to be an old woman, half-remembered as Manet's vulgar *Olympia*, forgotten as a painter.

For now, her mother welcomes the irregular envelopes that are sent to her from Paris. She sits by the fire, surrounded by shelves of empty milk crocks, and she thinks fondly of her daughter who works as a servant in the city and always sends home what she can.

A Seatown Affair

They meet in the casino, though this place resembles neither an Italianate dance-hall nor a flashy gaming-house. It's more of an amusement arcade really; a dim barn lolling on the promenade, the interior wrapped in a fog of dampness, cigarette smoke and Mars bar sweetness.

There are women here, perched like birds in front of one-armed bandits. They pull at the machines as if they are slovenly husbands and there's no possibility of finding any enjoyment with them. They hold flowerpots brimming with coins and they pause only to stub out their cigarettes; another few minutes knocked off their lives.

Their fingers must stink, muses Annie. She waits for Kieran to appear through the glass doors that look out over Mutton Island to a dark finger of County Clare. The rain is roiling in torrents and there is not much of Black Head to be seen.

The women's eyes move from the machines anytime the doors open. When another of their acquaintances joins the line, a greeting chant begins and their words are clipped, each syllable holding the same weight:

'Howya Caitriona. How's the form?'

'Howya Josephine. I'm grand, now, grand'.

'Jesus, you're looking great'.

The new arrival slings the strap of her handbag across her body and stuffs the greedy maw of the machine with coppers.

Kieran is late. Annie sits in the café area, sipping at scalding tea from a polystyrene cup. She has bitten away the rim of the cup and it bears the frilled pattern of her teeth. The games machines compete, whirring jingles and flashing colours. Kieran blusters through the door, his jacket wet, mouthing a 'Sorry' as he struggles with the wind-lashed door.

Annie's stomach flip-flops. She lowers her eyes, momentarily embarrassed at what they are doing. The bandit women's eyes flick over Kieran, and the machines gorge and purge noisily.

'Hi', he breathes, into Annie's mouth. His mouth is cool and damp. She pulls his head closer, pushing her tongue between his lips. He laughs. 'I take it you missed me?'

Kieran is of one generation and she is of another. He is wrinkled, salt-and-pepper-haired. They sit with their heads almost touching, feeling the air heat up between them. He takes her hand and rubs her fingers, each one in turn.

'What made you pick this place?'

'Just look around', he says, 'who'd see us here?'

'I suppose', she replies, thinking it unlikely that anyone she knows has ever been here.

Kieran's smile stretches slowly, slicing his face and lightening it.

'How's Caroline?' she enquires, and he winces.

'Fine', he says, folding his brow into a concertina of lines. 'How are *you*, more to the point?'

His wife, up until seven months ago, was all they had in common. Caroline is a work colleague of Annie's friend, and Kieran, her husband, flirted with Annie whenever they met. Caroline is ten years younger than Kieran. She is an attractive and committed career woman. They don't have sex. Annie is ten years younger than Caroline. She likes her in a semi-admiring way, but she is distant from her in many things.

'So, what about Saturday night?' says Annie, trying to sound light. 'My Swiss friends arrive on Thursday and they're really looking forward to meeting you'.

'I haven't forgotten', he says gently, 'I *will* be there. Will I bring anything?'

'Just yourself'.

She has known him for three years. She has hugged him close in front of his wife. She has even been to parties at his house, drunk from his glassware, used his bathroom. She knows well the stretch of the skin over his bones and the hazel-flecks in the brown eyes that have followed her around many rooms.

Gabi and Christian are consoling. They sit at the dinner table and offer all kinds of platitudes, unwrapping each one hopefully like savoured sweets.

'Maybe he got held up at work'.

He doesn't work on Saturdays.

'Maybe his child is sick and he can't get away'.

His only son is fourteen and he stays as far away from Kieran as possible.

'Maybe he didn't realise it was *this* weekend'.

He realised alright, he knew.

'Poor Annie', they croon, 'poor Annie'.

She is inconsolable and tears splat into her salad. Her friends are understanding when she gets drunk and they have to undress her for bed. Once alone she alternates between angry crying and room-spinning, heaving sickness. The night passes without the phone ringing.

They meet in the basement of a pub. It's a lofty cavern hung with brocade drapes and the walls are stencilled with *fleur-de-lys*. One wall is dominated by a painting of a swimming pool. It feels as if you are in the pool, an ice-blue ceiling of water stretching over your head. Annie stares into the painting and tries to let the calming water wash over her. She rattles ice cubes in the bottom of her glass.

There is a smell of bleach – an overwhelming masculine smell – and she notices that the floor has recently been mopped. She is alone in the downstairs bar, but the voices of the afternoon drinkers up above drift like renegade smoke spirals down to where she sits. She hears the whoosh of the revolving door upstairs; a blast of sea air arrives in with its turning. Soon Kieran appears and stands in front of her table. Annie keeps her head down. Kieran has a habit of swaying from side to side before he speaks, as if his words can't emerge without the comfort of a rhythm. She leaves him floundering for a few moments.

'Well?' she intones.

'I'm sorry, Annie', he whispers.

She won't easily thaw. She swirls the ice in her glass and pokes at the lemon wedge with her finger. She sucks the bitterness from the crescent of fruit and eyes Kieran. He leans forward, his hands splayed on the table. Then he sits down and pulls her to him, his side to her side. She lets her head fall to his shoulder.

'Caroline had organised a night out in Maria and Tom's. Either she never told me or I completely forgot. I couldn't get away from them to ring. I'm sorry'.

'I felt like an idiot', she says.

They fall onto each other. His hands roam inside her T-shirt and they become unaware of the smoke and muffled TV noises from the upstairs bar.

They meet in a drab hotel on the Dublin Road. She checks in alone and walks the corridors to find the room, breathing the fusty smells that linger everywhere. The room is stuck in a time warp with its floral carpet and stained bedspread.

The bathroom's grouting is black from years of human grime and careless cleaning. She is disappointed.

She sits in the foyer, her eyes trailing across the ash littered table and crumb-splattered floor. She checks the wineglass for thumb and lip prints before pouring from a miniature bottle. It's a New World red, but it is bitter and there is an oily film on the wine's surface. Still, her first gulp is a big one as she is looking forward to the heat it will bring to her throat and belly.

The radio behind the reception desk spews the evening news: '... drugs haul with an estimated street value of three million euro ...'

She flicks through a crumpled *Herald*. An elderly couple sit on a sofa nearby, their day's shopping strewn in bags at their feet. They drink covetously and she wonders if this is a cherished routine: a couple of drinks in the hotel after their Saturday shopping trip.

Kieran heads straight for the bar when he arrives, forty minutes late. Annie is bored sitting in this crummy foyer with only yesterday's newspaper for company. Her fingers are ink-blackened and, on a trip to the bathroom, she notices that her teeth are green from the wine. She feels a bit drunk. He sits down on a stool opposite her.

'What's wrong with this chair here beside me?' she asks. He tuts and sighs. 'Oh, stay where you are, if it's such a big deal', she snaps. Kieran is restless, quiet, very unlike himself. 'OK, what is it?' she asks, sure that he is going to say he can't stay away for the night. He rolls his whiskey around on his tongue, and looks straight at her with something like contempt. 'What's wrong, Kieran?' she says.

'Nothing', he says, and smiles with an effort that is obvious. 'Come on, let's sit in the lounge'.

They talk of ordinary things: work problems, a film they had both watched on RTÉ, what they might have for dinner tonight. The atmosphere lightens, but there is still a weight in the air that swings, pendulum like, back and forth between them.

Their lovemaking is detached. There has been a coldness about Kieran all evening and Annie knows that there are things being left unsaid. She snuggles into his chest and his fingers comb through her hair. She falls asleep and, in the half-light of morning, wakes to find Kieran sitting up against the headboard, staring at her. She struggles to shake the night from her body, but before she is fully awake, he speaks: 'Caroline is pregnant'.

Annie lies back on the pillow, scrunching her eyes shut, wishing she was still asleep, hoping that she is, knowing that she's not. She gets dressed and leaves without saying a single word.

They meet in an ice-cream parlour. It's one of a chain and it's bright and warm. The smells are sweet and fruity, and Annie is enjoying a mix of juices blended in a tall glass. Her drink is called a Mangomania, which she finds amusing.

Black Head is clearly visible today, outlined in navy blue against a lowering sky. From her perch in the window she can see rain clouds scudding across the bay from where cliffs are hidden beyond the headland. The sun is fingering rays of light through the clouds and they sparkle in lines on the churning sea.

The door heaves wide and a breeze licks its way through the opening. Even with her belly curved high, Caroline manages to stride through the doorway.

'Hi, Annie', she says, air-kissing behind each of her ears. 'I'm delighted you rang. I'm so bored at home these days. Just waiting, waiting, waiting!'

She pats her belly.

Annie smiles at her.

'Oh, I've just been dying to see you, Caroline. It's been absolutely ages, hasn't it?'

'I suppose it has', she agrees, frowning a little as if she can't remember or care less.

'And we've so much in common, you and I', laughs Annie, 'more than you realise'.

Caroline looks at her for a moment, her pretty features hardened, before turning to the waitress who is waiting to take her order. When Caroline has finished ordering, Annie speaks.

'So', she begins, 'how's Kieran? The father-to-be. Happy and well, I hope?'

'Kieran? Oh, he's grand, Annie, just fine. I'm exhausted, of course!'

Rain begins to teem against the window and an angry Atlantic wind careens its way along the street, causing drivers to move more slowly through the belting blasts. The bunting and flags that were hung for last week's festival snap and crack in the squall. Puddles swell from the kerbs into the roadway.

Annie continues talking and Caroline sits on the other side of the table, her peachy skin paling as her mouth forms a shocked 'O'. Her hands move to cradle the swell of her abdomen and her breath leaves her mouth in short spurts. Annie sits opposite her and she smiles; a tight, mean curve of a smile that has lain dormant inside her, waiting for this moment to arrive.

The River Flows On

Going home. The hit of it. The bring-you-down feelings. Despite your happy childhood. Everything's the same, but changed. You're like a giant in a familiar land; nowadays you find you must climb over the bushes instead of through them.

The gooseberry bush has been pulled from your favourite field. You circle the spot where it used to be, and miss the bitter bite of the downy globes, their tough sour skins. The apple tree you once fell from has been felled. You remember the thunk as you hit the ground and the dizziness you felt when you stood up. Two pines grow taller than you. Two pines that shouldn't exist because they don't share your history. The snowberry bush stands waiting for the snap and fizz of berries bursting between tiny fingers.

But the river flows on. Muddy and pungent and threatening. You call to mind the foul weedy stink you took home with you whenever you swam in it. The broken-bottle glass on the riverbed. The threat of whirlpools and dangerous currents. The drownings.

It's all a part of you. You own this part of the Liffey. This side of the bank, at least. The other side is a wilderness, as uncharted and deep as a tropical forest. The herons and the swans that wade and glide on this side of the riverbank are familiar to you. You know them. On the other bank lies a choking wilderness. Wolves slink through the trees, revealing only a silvery flank or the flash of a gilded eye. There are bodies caught in the rushes.

You pick wild garlic and chew on the stems, spitting the mulched clumps into the grass. You visit the ruins of the church, lifting the viny curtain from the entrance and bending to step inside. The smell of death mingled with damp earth sends you reeling. The corpse of a wild cat lies rotting among the stones, its mottled fur a heaving nest of maggots. So you turn and leave. You return to the river's edge to watch the swirling dance of leaves and twigs that are caught behind a fallen tree, their water journey come to a halt.

And you think of him. The workaholic aggressive that you chose from among all the men you knew. He who thinks you know nothing of his betrayals. His whitewashing. His reams of excuses. And you realise he doesn't know the first thing about you. Or the last. He doesn't know that the river is part of you, and that you are part of it.

So, you heave yourself into the water with a small laugh. Hoping for a cleansing. Or a whirlpool. You belong to the rushing water, its eddies and gushes. You delight in the undertow, the pull of the current when you glide past the spot where the mill race meets the flow. The riverweed wraps its velvety fingers around your ankles and slides up your thighs. The dankness engulfs your hair, and the metallic dirt of the water slips between your teeth, cramming itself into your waiting lungs. You feel yourself fill to the brim, and your head aches, but then there is a curious calm, so you smile.

You slip – quiet now – towards Chapelizod, past tree-lined banks where fishermen are lost in their own reveries, and they don't notice you passing. Your arms float out from your sides like wings and you spin a little, your knees bent. Your shoes have found their rest on the sludge of the riverbed, and your wrists have picked up a trail of riverwrack bracelets.

If you were capable of thought now, you would be enjoying yourself. The slow pace of the water; the lift and fall of your co-operating limbs; the rushing hustle of the trees as you pass. Most of all you would be enjoying the view. The clouds scudding overhead in the unlit sky. Your own part of the river ebbing away and away while you float on through unknown territory. You would appreciate the patterns made by the half-light slipping through the canopy of leaves when you veer close to the riverbank. You would like the fact that the far bank is nearer to you now than your own, and that the wolves are sitting in easy groups, watching your progress.

You are languid now, cradled by the river that has rocked you to sleep. Your pace is slowing and the smile is falling from your lips. One foot snags on the branch of a fallen tree, and you spin for a moment before halting in the stagnant water gathered behind the trunk. The scurf that washes back and forth on the surface coats your hair. When your head is momentarily submerged by the ebb and flow, a twig settles itself between your open teeth. An eel glides through the crook of your arm, and hovers for a moment over the curve of your belly, before flickering on in search of food.

Restrained now, your movements become more sluggish. Your skin has taken on a pearly sheen and your arms lie limp. This is not the freedom you had hoped for, you didn't mean to be stayed so soon. Water skids and slides around and about and over you. You remain an unwieldy lump of flotsam, bobbing and ducking in the shadow of the fallen tree.

Until your absence is noted and, with the quickening dusk worry sets in, and efforts are made to find you. To bring you back.

And the river flows on.

LIFE WAS SO WONDERFUL

We sat in a huddle in the Pullman Lounge of the B&I Lines ferry, our duffel coats damp from our walk around the deck. We could see the last edges of Dublin and the grey misery of the Irish Sea through the windows that lined the walls. Outside, the seagulls were flying backwards. Daddy and Granny had seats, but me and my sisters sat on our bags and tried to keep our balance while the boat lunged and bobbed into the waves. Deirdre's face was as pale as raw turnip.

A fella who was slumped in a seat across from us sang along to his transistor. 'The Logical Song' blasted from it and I watched his sunburnt face concentrating on getting the words right. Sometimes, when he didn't know the lines of the song, he just made word shapes with his mouth. But when he came to a bit that he knew, he'd sing those words very loud. He turned up the volume. The red-raw skin of his forehead didn't go with his sandy hair which was scraped into a ponytail with an elastic band. His face became all serious when he sang the words 'Please tell me who I am', and he tapped out the rhythms of the song on the arm of his seat.

An old couple sitting a few seats away were filled with drink. They must have been in the pub on the docks before coming on board. The bar and the duty free shop on the ferry had just opened. Me and Ciara had looked in the door at all the giant bars of chocolate on the shelves beside the bottles and fags, until Daddy told us to come away out of that. I watched as the old man laid his head in the greasy V of the woman's chest and closed his eyes. She sighed and let her arm drop around his shoulder. Her head jerked and she burped, excusing herself in a mumble. Then she closed her eyes too and her head lolled and bucked as if her neck found it too heavy to hold up.

I looked at Daddy. He had grooves on his forehead and every now and then he let out a low moan. I was chewing the ends of my hair, something Mammy always told us not to do. 'You'll get a ball of hair in your stomach', she would say, 'and it'll strangle you'. Then she would slap your hand away from the spit-soaked hair and you would miss its salty taste. But you would suck on it again when she wasn't looking. Daddy didn't say to stop. He didn't say 'Take that hair out of your mouth', or, 'You'll have it like rats' tails', the way Mammy would have.

'This is great, isn't it, Dad?' I said.

He stared at me and then he turned to Granny and the two of them laughed. Not happy laughs, though. Deirdre snorted and dropped her head between her knees so she wouldn't have to look at any of us.

'It *is* great', said Granny suddenly. 'Aren't you such lucky children to be going to England on your holidays? It's more than your father ever did as a child. Or me for that matter. You'll have a lovely time on the beach'.

Daddy said nothing; he looked across the heads of all the people in the damp lounge at the murky windows of the ferry.

I thought about our last holiday, the only other one we had ever had. It was more of a day out really. We had all gone on the train to Dublin to take a Ghost Tour on a special bus. Mammy wore her good hat and she was smiling and she squeezed Daddy's hand as we stood in the queue on O'Connell Street. We chose seats on the top deck and the bus rolled out of the city and headed south along the coast road.

'Looks like we're heading back the way we came, girls', Daddy called to us. He was grinning and pointing things out to Mammy.

Deirdre looked at me and crossed her eyes. None of us spoke as the bus trundled on towards our hometown and disappointment wrapped itself around us like a fog. We ate our picnic at our own kitchen table. Mammy's hat was still pinned to her hair and she had a grim look on her face. Then Daddy laughed. He laughed out loud. His eyes watered and his face reddened and he nearly choked on his sandwich. He shook and hooted, belting his hand against the table until Mammy slapped him on the back.

'That's enough, Tom', she snapped, but Daddy laughed more.

Then Mammy started to giggle and Daddy grabbed her out of her chair and danced her around the kitchen, singing 'Cushy Butterfield' into her hat. We took the Ghost Tour bus back up to Dublin that afternoon to get the train back home again.

'We've paid for the bloody trip, we might as well take it!' Daddy had declared.

'Don't be cursing in front of the girls, Tommy', said Mammy crossly, but really everything was alright because she only ever called him Tommy when she was in good form.

'I want Mammy', said Ciara. Daddy yanked her so hard by the arm that she fell off the bag that she was perched on. She stared up at him, her small face wobbling.

Daddy stood up and shouted, 'Come on, we'll all go for a walk around the deck'.

Deirdre looked up from the book she was reading. She scowled at the rest of us.

'You stay here, Deirdre, and mind the seats and the bags', said Granny.

The four of us trooped out onto the soaked deck and held onto the rail to stop ourselves from blowing away. The boat lumbered through the water. A squall whipped my hood down and slapped my hair into my eyes. Granny tried to tighten the knot of her headscarf and toppled backwards onto Ciara and me. Daddy held onto Granny's arm after that and we battled our way around the prow of the boat, scrunching up our eyes against the spray and the rain. The gusts blew us through a door on the far side of the deck into the calm and hum of the ship's insides.

'Let's eat our lunch', said Granny when we got back to the lounge, because she couldn't think of anything else to do.

It was only eleven o'clock and we had been on the boat less than an hour but Daddy unpacked the sandwiches. They were smoked ham on white batch, because it was a special occasion. Granny poured MiWadi into smelly plastic cups. The orange was warm and Ciara was about to complain when Deirdre gave her a warning puck.

'What?!' screeched Ciara, glaring at Deirdre and rubbing at her arm.

'Oh just shut up!' roared Daddy, and we looked at him, amazed, because as well as chewing on your hair, telling someone to shut up was another thing you're never supposed to do.

We ate our sandwiches without speaking. I rolled the ham around on my tongue, to get the full benefit of its smoky flavour, and looked up from under my eyelids at

Daddy. The ferry roiled on towards Liverpool and we sat in the Pullman Lounge, lurching and swaying with the movement of the sea, not saying or thinking much at all.

Our rooms were on the top floor of the hotel in Blackpool. Daddy and Granny had one room and we had the other. I had to share a bed with Ciara. Her body was hard and uncomfortable and I hated lying beside her. There was a window set high into the wall above our bed and at night I could see the dark steel outline of the tower, all lit up and lovely against a navy sky.

Our days were full of food; a fried breakfast in the morning led to an early fish-and-chip lunch in a café and on to dinner at the hotel in the evening. Our waiter was the sandy-haired singer from the ferry and he liked to flash his eyes at Deirdre as he set our plates down. His name was Steve and he would sing as he served us, all about other people who were singing so happily and joyfully.

We devoured chops and baked beans; poked at egg mayonnaise and sloppy oozing beetroot; marvelled at a dessert of half a peach, skinned and floating in syrup, that looked exactly like a raw egg. Ciara put her napkin on her head, thinking it was a hat. Daddy slapped her hand and she cried like a kitten.

'Tom!' said Granny. 'Don't cry, pet', she whispered to Ciara, pulling her onto her lap.

Between meals we traipsed up and down the Golden Mile, our bare legs stung by the sand that blew in from the beach. The air all around was drenched with the smells of popcorn, candyfloss and chips. We slipped coins into games machines, hoping for a win. Deirdre wouldn't play the slots and she sulked along behind the rest of us wherever we went. Twice a day she lost us and made her way back to the hotel to read.

'She's really starting to annoy me', said Daddy, when we sat in a café on the North Pier after losing Deirdre in the creepy darkness of Louis Tussaud's waxworks.

'She's fifteen', said Granny, 'she wants to be on her own'.

Daddy grunted and we finished our chips while looking out at the rain and waves beating against the black sand.

Deirdre went missing on our last evening. The evening we'd chosen to visit the tower which the brochure said had 'floor after floor of indoor entertainment, which even the great British weather cannot spoil!' Me and Ciara put on our best dresses and Granny tied new ribbons in our hair. We sat side by side on our bed while Daddy went looking for Deirdre. Granny snapped the clasp of her handbag open and shut, open and shut. Her mouth was gripped into a lined 'O'.

'What will we look at first in the tower, Granny?' asked Ciara.

'What? Oh, we'll probably go right up to the top and work our way down'.

'Down to the Tower Circus, right at the bottom!' said Ciara.

I thought about telling Granny that I'd seen Deirdre earlier with Steve, the sandy-haired waiter. She had stepped into the two-person lift with him and he'd put his arm around her shoulder. Deirdre had seen me watching and she stuck out her tongue at me. As the lift door closed I'd heard Steve's voice still on the same old song, singing something about radicals and criminals. I couldn't understand what it was about; or why he seemed to like it so much.

Daddy came back to our room. It was dusk dark. He'd been gone a long time and Ciara had fallen asleep on the bed. I'd made myself stay awake.

'There's no sign of her', he said, 'I'm after looking all over the place'.

Granny looked worried.

'We'll have to call the Guards, Tom. The police'.

'I saw her with Steve', I whispered.

'What? What did you say?' Daddy said.

'She's with Steve'.

'Steve? Steve? Who in God's name is Steve?' he said.

'Calm down, Tom', said Granny.

Ciara woke up and tried to rub the heaviness from her eyes.

'Jesus Christ', said Daddy, 'it's that waiter, isn't it? It's that ponce with the ponytail who never stops singing. That's who she's with! I'll kill her. I'll bloody well kill her. She's like her mother. Just like her mother!'

'Ah now, Tom, the girls are listening', said Granny, putting her hand on Daddy's arm.

They went into their own room then, and Ciara and I got into bed still wearing our dresses. The lights of the tower winked down at us through the window high up on the wall. It took a long time to fall asleep.

Early the next morning we took the coach from Blackpool back to Liverpool. Deirdre's eyes were puffy and she refused to speak, even to Granny. Daddy didn't sit with us when we got onto the boat. He stood in the corridor waiting for the bar to open. The ferry plunged through the water towards Dublin and we sat in the Pullman Lounge, lurching and swaying with the movement of the sea, not saying or thinking much at all.

PIG ALLEY

Until you were eight, and even though you didn't know it, you lived in the red-light district of your hometown. Though that's a grand name for what was a few kip houses and sheebeens on grubby streets. The area was known by some as Pig Alley, and the story went that a local man had once visited Paris's Pigalle, with it's red-sailed windmill and high-kicking girls, and had brought back his own version of the name.

'Just another Pig Alley, that's what this place is', he'd said.

The streets bulged with tenements and your parents decided to settle there until something better came along. You shared one cobwebby room and remained an only child; Mammy's little boy.

On warm days the women tumbled out onto the streets and lounged in lazy clumps. Sometimes, at Essie Snade's house, they would place a gramophone in the window and play the same songs over and over. The whole of Pig Alley filled with the lilt of 'Papa Piccolino' and the women sang along in warbled, twittery voices, hefting the crank when the music slowed.

To you they were your neighbours, though you did know there was something different about them. You would hear people saying things you didn't understand. They used words like 'Madam' and 'kip-house'. They said them in a way that made you feel dirty and you would curl in on yourself when you heard those things.

You once asked the one they called Fat Annie where her husband lived. She was sunning herself on the street and her belly wobbled even as she sat.

'Where's Mr Fat Annie?' you said. 'Does he live in a house with loads of men?'

Annie spluttered and gasped and bellowed, slapping at her phlegm-filled chest and swiping at her streeling eyes. You stared at her jiggling bosom, waiting for the ash of her cigarette to fall to powder on the cobbles. She was big every way and you used to think if she fell into the pea-green murk of the Liffey, she would torpedo to the bottom in a long swift dive.

'Jesus, Mary and Joseph', she said, 'I've enough men coming around to this house to last me a lifetime, son, the last thing I want is a bloody husband!'

You walked away, glancing back until Annie came and hugged you and handed over a few warm bullseyes.

'Ah, you poor little divil', she crooned.

They were country women mostly, hiding their knowledge of animals and weather among the smokestacks and din of the city. They carried their rolls of fat prettily, and they always looked clean in white blouses and floral shawls. You loved their powdery smells and their cocky kindnesses. You would sit in their laps while they fed you bits of chocolate. Even moody Miss Brady called you her 'little loveen' when she found you playing outside her door. Miss Brady locked her girls in during the day, and they would shout down to you as you passed.

'Come here, pet, run to Murray's and get me a few fags. They're me one pleasure. Here's the money, you can keep the change'.

Then they'd lower a can carefully to the ground so that it wouldn't tip and knock the coins into the grating on the street.

On Sundays Miss Brady would line her girls out for Mass, and they would troop ahead of the rest of you to the church on the quay, their hats pulled low. You would meet your Granny on the corner, so that you could go to Mass with her, and she would always say the same thing. 'Look at them. Poor unfortunate girls'.

Your Daddy would grind his teeth. 'They're hardly as unfortunate as some', he would say.

Granny would snort, and adjust her handbag. She knew Daddy was cranky on Sunday mornings, so she never made another comment. That is until the following week. You always defended them too, but you did it quietly, in your mind.

Granny had a small tortoise mouth that never seemed to unpucker. She didn't hug you, but would say 'There you are' as if she couldn't figure out who you were. Mammy didn't come to Mass with you and Daddy because she and Granny had differences. When they met they would stand either side of Daddy, snapping at one another and pulling him between them on an invisible rope.

After Mass, Daddy would nod at the girls from Miss Brady's house and smoke a cigarette. One of the girls always caught his eye the longest. Her name was Rose and, like the rest, she was starting to get fat. She wore hooped earrings that flashed, and she had small white teeth. She would smile at Daddy, her eyes lifted up from underneath the brim of her hat. Granny would humph and tut and say nothing. When Daddy had finished his smoke he would go to the pub and you would walk with Granny as far as Pig Alley, then run away from her as she called 'Bye, so' after you in her watery voice.

Soon after you had started noticing Rose exchanging looks with your Daddy, she cornered you on the street. She was milk-pale and jittery, looking over her shoulder towards Miss Brady's. The house was locked up and you guessed that she wasn't supposed to be out at all.

'Will you bring a message to your Daddy?' she said, squeezing your arm.

'What?' you answered, trying to pull her fingers off your arm, but she pinched harder, holding you away from her.

'The cut of ye', she sniped, 'you'll never be as big as your Daddy'.

Fat Annie came out of her house and called across the street, 'What are you doing with him?'

'Nothing, Missus, he's just going on a message for me, aren't ye, pet?' said Rose.

'Yes', you said. Fat Annie paused, then went back inside and shut the door.

'Come on', said Rose. She dragged you down the street, her face grim. At Boyle's pub, she pushed you into the snug. You had never been inside a pub before and you gawped at the low lights and the spit-laden sawdust that decorated the floor. The snug was empty and she sat you across from her with a glass of lemonade. You felt you shouldn't be there, but you wanted the lemonade so you stayed. Rose seemed to calm down and she showed her small teeth in a smile.

'Now', she said, 'is that nice, is it?'

You agreed that it was, but you decided to get it into you quickly in case she took it back. You looked at the yellow flowers cascading down the edges of her grey shawl and wished that you could get one like that for your Mammy.

'I'm eight', you said.

Rose was sipping at an amber whiskey. Her skin was stretched across her bones.

'Eight, is it?' she said. 'You only look about six'.

'I *am* eight' you said, 'I'm not some babby of six!'

Rose laughed and, after a minute, you laughed with her.

'No, you're no babby', she said, 'but I'd say you like them, little babbies. How would you like a brother? I can get one for you', she whispered. 'In fact, I have one right here'.

You looked at her and thought she must be a bit mad. You were the only two people in that snug, the dust motes flying through a shaft of light between you. Rose stared at you with slitted eyes. She drained her glass and lunged across the table, knocking your lemonade to the floor as she clutched your jumper in her fist.

'Yes, I have one right here. A little bastard babby', she spat, letting go of you so that you fell backwards. 'Tell that to your Daddy', she hissed.

You ran from the snug and you could hear her laugh follow you out through the door.

There had been a raid the night before you found the dead baby in the alley. Mammy made you wear your boots when you went out to play because the cobbles were bright with glass. The police were supposed to break all the bottles they found inside, but Daddy said that they broke only a few and took the rest back to the barracks with them, the greedy bastards.

'The Madams will be raging', Mammy said happily.

Outside you picked your way through the glass, the brown boots pinching at your feet from every side. You slid your finger in around the ankle rim but the boots were stiff. You decided to take them off until it was time to go in and you looked around for a place to hide them. You streaked along the back of Miss Brady's house looking for a spot where the boots might remain safe for a couple of hours. You noticed a pile of brown rags heaped against the wall and you poked at them with your foot to make sure there wasn't a rat hiding in under them, ready to jump out and bite your neck. There was something wrapped up in the rags. You pulled at the corner of the bundle and it unravelled. You pulled again. Out rolled the tiny body of a baby. You stood gawping at it for a couple of seconds, unsure of what your eyes were telling you.

The baby's skin was waxy and there was a collection of blue marks on the bulge of its belly; a little black stump stood where the belly button should be. The baby's head was capped with small rivers of brown blood and its arms were curled into its chest as if it was trying to keep itself warm. You stumbled backwards, staring at the baby's perfect features and cold skin. Then you turned and ran.

Your parents stayed up all that night, shouting in whispers. Mammy cried. The police had called to your door earlier, but you were sent off to play. You lay on your mattress in the dark listening to the angriness. You knew it was all your fault for finding the little baby behind Miss Brady's house. Mammy slapped Daddy hard on the face and you started to cry.

In the morning Mammy sat on the chair, her tea gone cold. There was no sign of Daddy. You stood in your vest in the chilly room, afraid to go near her. Her eyelids were swollen and her skin was blotched. Someone knocked on the door.

'There's a knock, Mammy', you said.

She didn't move, so you pulled on your trousers and answered it. One of Fat Annie's girls stood there, holding a tray covered with a cloth.

'That's for your Mammy, pet', she said, 'from Annie Corbally'.

'Thank you', you said.

You carried the heavy tray to where Mammy sat, still unmoving. You could smell cooked chicken and trickles of spit loosened on your tongue. You placed the tray on the table and lifted the cloth with one finger to peep underneath. Mammy jumped up and slapped your hand away. She grabbed the tray and tipped it into the fireplace, cloth and all.

'Bitches!' she shouted and you jumped.

The tray sat in the ashes; the back end of the roast chicken all smutted and the milk from an up-ended jug puddling in the grate.

Daddy came back after a few days. From then on, while you still lived in that room, you slept in the big bed with Mammy, while Daddy took your place on the mattress near the fireplace. A few months later you moved out to a small house in Terenure, where the yew trees stalked their way up towards the Dublin Mountains and the light was clean and pure. Your neighbours, and all the years in Pig Alley, were never mentioned after that, and the air between your parents softened as they moved slowly back towards each other again.

KICKING UP MURDER

Her mammy has fallen asleep so Anna leaves the door open a little and skitters off down the hall. Then she tiptoes back to look through the slit and feel the cool air that slides through and makes tears collect in her eye. She watches her mother lying in the bed. She is milk-pale; a flowered turban sits on her head, hiding the wisps of hair that she's been left with. Her eyes open then close again slowly. They flick open once more when she grunts and moves her body to make herself more comfortable. Anna thinks that her mammy's eyes look bigger than ever since her eyelashes have disappeared. The bed sighs under her. It's granda's old bed; the sick bed.

Anna moves her eye closer to the gap in the doorway and thinks of the joke mammy tells: When is a door not a door? When it's a jar.

It's the only joke her mammy knows and she always laughs when she tells it. Anna laughs too, though sometimes the laugh nearly turns to crying because she is so happy to be with her mother, telling jokes and laughing. Sometimes when mammy is pleased like that Anna squeezes her hand and touches the wrinkly bits beside her eyes with her fingers. Mammy calls the lines around her eyes crow's feet and that makes Anna laugh.

'They're not crow's feet!'

'They are, they are, would you just look at them!'

Mammy used to have white hair, yellowy-white like the inside of a potato, but now she has a fuzz on her head. It feels soft.

Mary, the nurse, won't be coming today. Saturday is her day off. Anna is glad. She has to keep out of the way and be quiet when Mary is in the house.

'What are you up to?' The voice of her father drags her back to now. She jumps back from the crack in the door. 'Will you ever leave her in peace?' he says, his face pulling against itself in anger.

He's glaring at her and he fumes through his nose in short puffs, like the horses in the hill field. Anna stares back at him, unused to this bad temper. She walks away, trying not to let her sandals clatter on the tiles and she slips out through the front door to sit in the garden and suck up the smell of the lilacs.

Her sister, Rose, comes to collect her. Rose is older, a grown woman really, married to Tom and all. Anna hears the roll of the tyres on the gravel and the crunch of the handbrake as she pulls up. It's late and she has been waiting, wearing an old nightdress of mammy's and her own slippers with their band of pink fur.

'What have you got on you?' Rose says, when she sees Anna standing in the hall. She shoves past her to where their father is waiting. 'Is she a lot worse?' He nods and leads Rose down the hall to stand at the sitting-room door and stare into the gloomy room where his wife lies collapsed in the bed, her breathing loud. 'Oh my God', her sister whispers and turns away to walk out to the car.

The nightdress Anna wears is too long for her and she feels old-fashioned and fancy as she bunches the skirts in her hands and lifts the ends high to step into the car. 'Do I look like a princess?' she would say to her niece if she were there, but Noreen is not in the car, she's already at home in her bed. Noreen is only three years younger than Anna but she is her niece. She could treat her bossy and make a big thing of being her auntie, but she doesn't bother.

The engine of Rose's car throttles and hasps to life and a drone like a hive of metallic bees hums under the bonnet. It's a familiar buzz – their father drives the same car and there's comfort in the engine's thrum.

When they get to Rose and Tom's house Anna is sent straight up to bed. She will have to climb into the feet-end beside Noreen and try to fall asleep under the foreign weight of the blankets, listening to the city traffic passing behind the curtains. Her niece snuffles and grumbles when she opens the door.

'It's only me. Me, Anna', she whispers into the darkness as she climbs into the far end of the bed.

The blankets are a lumpy huddle collapsing over the edges of the bed as if a huge wind had ploughed through the room and mangled them. Streaks of light fan out over the ceiling, the headlights of the passing cars that always make their way into this room. The lights show off the patches of mildew that blossom over the wallpaper. Anna lies back and stares at the shapes on the wall.

She wishes for the dirty smell of her own pillow and the hush of the weir below the house where the river rushes over it to get to the bay. When she's not at home she always misses the small things, like the smell in the bathroom – a mixture of lavender and pee. Rose's house smells like stale onions. Anna misses the sounds of her own house too, like the lights being switched on and off in the rooms downstairs, each one different. The switch in the kitchen has a short, sharp snap; the one in the sitting room, where her mother now sleeps, has a tinny rasp. You need to fiddle with that one to get the light to come on at all. There's a knack.

Anna's mind drifts, the patterned wallpaper looms over her and she sees her mother's face. Mammy doesn't smile; her face is set and hard, not like herself at all. Anna thinks that her mammy's sickness is hot and creeping like a cartoon devil. It's red and spiky and sly. She mulls over its shape and the more she pictures it the more it changes. She sees it as a trap, a black hole, a well with no bottom. It's a sickness that swallows up the body, sucks the good out of it and spits back up the bones and the meat. Then the person lies empty and airless like the cast off skin of a worm. Anna's eyes close, then flutter open again, just like her Crolly doll when she rocks it back and forth to listen to the click of its eyelids.

She falls asleep.

Anna hates Sundays, the dragged out feeling; the stickiness of steamed up windows from the dinner that's cooked too early, before the house has a chance to warm up to itself. The adults are always crabby on Sundays, uncomfortable with the tight laziness of the day.

Herself and Noreen have a fit of the giggles at Mass, during the flat bit between the Creed and the Our Father. The church is wide and bright, with a slab of marble for an altar. The priest mumbles through the words, changing his voice only at the end of each prayer, hardly ever lifting his eyes to the people.

The girls sit one row in front of Rose and Tom on a shiny pine pew that's lorded over by a mournful statue of Jesus. Anna's face is as red as a poppy. The laughter bursts out of her mouth in a shower of spits and she's afraid. Rose is sniping at them, pucking them between the shoulder blades from behind. She can see them shaking; they're grabbing each other's hands, tears streeling down their faces, egging each other on. They calm down, then one of them forces out a giggle and they're off again. Their jaws are sore so they pinch their cheeks to try to stop laughing.

Rose grabs Anna and drags her from the church, leaving Noreen behind. She pulls her past all the people, out through the porch to the cemented-over grounds where she shakes her by the arm.

'Poor mammy', she bawls, 'poor mammy and look at you'.

'But', says Anna.

'Don't but me, young lady', screeches Rose. Rose is kicking up murder; shaking her by the shoulder and making her head wobble. She rasps her anger into Anna's face delivering the warm tang of coffee that always hangs on her breath. Anna turns her head away and her sister's fingers dig further into her shoulder, shaking her again. 'Do you know how sick mammy is, do you? Do you even care?'

There's no one to see the way she pulls at her, or to hear her bellowing the way a sick cow does. Everyone is still inside the church, praying. Standing and kneeling and sitting and praying. Passing the time.

Catherine can feel the strength leaving her, her body giving up its power. It's a vague, welcome feeling like the long slide into sleep. She lies, a long blanketed hump, in her father's old bed, the bed that wears death as casually as a worn sheet.

'Anna', she calls, wanting to tell her the things she should have been told all along.

She doesn't appear.

Catherine calls again but she can't be sure that her voice is loud enough or that she's saying the name properly. She starts to cry, a low whimper that barely gets past her lips. Her husband, Jimmy, strokes her head, unwrapping the floral turban from her head when he feels the heat of her skin under his fingers.

'It's alright, Cath', he croons, 'she's with Rose, she's alright'.

'Anna', she mumbles, her mouth working hard to form the name.

Jimmy sits beside her all night, his head flopping into sleep every so often. He leaves her only for the few minutes it takes to ring Mary, the nurse. He knows that Catherine's time is near. He also knows that she wants to tell Anna the truth, but he's not so sure. Anna's still very young and she's such a moody, dreamy kind of a child. How will she take it? It'll be hard enough on her when Catherine goes, he thinks. It has to be up to Rose in the end, it will be her call. *She'll* have to decide whether Anna should be told or not; after all there's her husband Tom, and Noreen to consider, too. Oh God, what will Tom say? Jimmy thinks. Sure, maybe he knows already.

He drops his head into his hands. Two girls, he thinks. Two girls and he can talk to neither of them. It might've been easier if he'd had a son.

Jimmy had wanted to tell Anna from the start, so that she'd always know, but Catherine and Rose thought different. He was always afraid that someone else would tell Anna. Someone at school or one of the neighbours' kids, maybe. He thinks that some of them know; they must know. People are not stupid; they're not easily fooled. Anyway, everyone should know who their mother is. And their father, for that matter.

Catherine stirs, low moans bleat from her throat, her lips are dry and yellow.

'Jimmy', she whispers, barely saying his name. *'Jmmmy'*.

Tears slide from the comers of her eyes and slip into her ears. He wipes them away carefully with the comer of a tissue.

'What is it, pet? Is there anything I can do, love?'

He kisses her forehead lightly. Catherine's breath shudders and her mouth opens. Jimmy sees that her tongue is coated with a pale scurf. She looks parched, he thinks. Parched and exhausted and ready to leave. He curls his fingers around her warm hand and lies his head on her arm.

Anna and Noreen are eating their cornflakes. Tom is standing at the kitchen counter sipping coffee and reading the newspaper. Rose is still in bed. The phone rings and Tom leaves his paper to answer it.

'We'll call down to Gemma's house when we've had our baths', Noreen says.

'OK', answers Anna, wondering if Gemma's mother will have baked buns. She makes them with currants and she lets you eat them when they're still hot, straight from the oven.

Tom is standing with his back to where the girls sit at the table. He is nodding, the phone held to his ear.

'Yes', he says, 'OK. I'll tell her now. I'm so sorry, Jimmy. OK. We'll see you in a while'.

Tom looks at Anna and Noreen, then he turns away. He plops the receiver back onto the hook and he stands for a minute pinching the bridge of his nose with his fingers. He sighs and makes his way up the stairs to where Rose lies resting in bed.

Anna and Noreen hear a soft wail. They look at each other and Noreen throws her eyes up to Heaven and giggles. She shovels a big spoonful of cornflakes into her mouth letting the milk dribble from her lips to make Anna laugh. She doesn't laugh. She stares at Noreen and waits.

Tom comes down the stairs and stands in the doorway.

'Girls', he says, 'girls, go on up to mammy'.

Neither of them move.

'Come on, Anna. Go upstairs to Rose, she has something she wants to tell you'.

Anna looks at him and he turns away from her and starts to clear the breakfast dishes from the table.

ANY MAN'S FANCY

The café wasn't open long and the windows sweated from the steaming hiss of the coffee machine. Peter gulped his tea and scoffed back a sausage roll. He looked out the window over Strathross harbour and the sea loch beyond. The oil dark water sloshed and seals bobbed their heads in the waves. He burped, folded the napkin that had cloaked his cutlery and swiped at his mouth and beard. He strode down the stairs, the checked shirt he wore fanning out behind him, and joined the queue at the take-away bakery counter. The new girl was there today; she had only been working in the place a couple of weeks. She wore a white headscarf tossed around her copper hair.

'Gimme a meat pastie, a tuna roll and two dream rings', Peter said, when it was his turn.

'Will I heat up the pastie for you?' asked the girl, an Antipodean lilt to her voice.

'No, don't bother, hen', he said. 'You're a long way from home'.

'I guess so'.

Peter could find work anywhere. In Quebec he sank below the earth and worked dark days as a miner. Missouri had him felling trees by the hundred and learning how to dry hardwood lumber. As an undertaker's assistant in Glasgow, he mastered the art of prettifying the dead. He lasted a few months in a tannery near

Cherbourg, not having made it very far from the boat, but went on to work in an Irish Bar near Lyons.

These days he did what he could: a week on Calum's boat, hauling for herring; the odd night in the bar in the Caledonia Hotel and this-and-that jobs for everyone in the village. He didn't like to go too far. He had to be near to Sheena, in case anything happened.

He swung out through the door onto Shore Street and headed up the brae to Alasdair Patterson's house where he was going to spend the day sanding wooden floors.

On Argyll Street, in the small timber house that was tucked behind a clump of tangled bushes, Sheena lay in the murky bedroom, her eyes closed. A butterfly tossed and bashed against the window, its wings folded and dusty. It got caught in a crease in the curtains and rested there, its feelers moving, testing the heaviness in the air.

Sheena lay on her back. Her arms were flush with her sides and her oaky plait of hair lay like a rope across the pillow. Her skin was the colour of lard, except for her eyelids which were two purple bruises bulging from her face. The blue dress she wore was long and its sleeves gripped at her wrists in a flurry of dull lace.

The butterfly unfolded itself, flaunting a patch of crimson that was as flashy as stained glass. Then it settled back onto the curtain, showing only the grey of its underwing. Sheena lay still.

Peter decided to go home before going out. Alasdair was having a 'do' in The Highlander for his wife's birthday and he'd invited him to join them.

'Aye, I'll come along. I'll just go home and get washed up, alright?'

He still had one of the dream rings he'd bought earlier. He'd been saving it for later but marching down the brae from Alasdair's house, with the wind filling his ears, he pulled the cake from the paper bag. He sat on a rock by the roadside looking at the clear outline of the headland opposite and the wash of the water around the loch. There'll be rain tonight, he thought.

He held the dream ring in his hand, marvelling at the pure white of the icing that was snowed over the top. Carefully he pulled the two halves apart and slid his tongue across the sweet baker's cream that had held it together. He ate the bottom half first, wanting to save the crunchy crack of the icing on the top for last. When he had finished, he pulled each of his fingers through his teeth, cleaning them of crumbs and stickiness. Then he hopped up from the rock and jogged home to Argyll Street.

There was new sweat on top of old sweat leaking through his shirt by the time he arrived at the house. He decided to have a lukewarm kettle-water bath rather than wait for the immersion to heat the water in the tank.

'I'm home, hen', he called towards the bedroom, knowing Sheena would be lying down. 'I'm away out tonight, if that's OK with you. Alasdair's having a party for his Missus in The Highlander. But I won't stay late, alright?' Peter popped his head around the bedroom door. 'There you are, my love', he whispered, gazing at her pale face.

He took some incense from the chest of drawers lit a long stick of it and blew on it until it glowed. Sheena didn't stir. He waved the incense around in the air to tamp down the smell that had started to invade the room. He went into the bathroom and splashed the hot water from the kettle into the bath. He sat in a puddle of water to sponge the day from his body. He loved the feeling of the water lifting the grit from his skin after hard work. He sang while he soaped his beard and hair.

'Green grow the rushes, oh, green grow the rushes oh, oh, oh, the sweetest hours that e'er I spent, were spent among the lasses, oh'.

Working in Woolworth's suited Sheena fine, though she wasn't so sure about Glasgow. The other girls in the shop were nice enough, but they all had mothers and sisters and boyfriends to go home to and they weren't looking for new friends. Before she met Peter she spent most evenings watching TV in her flat in Hill Head. The odd night she'd trip down to a small cinema off Buyers Road and lose sight of her life in the darkness.

Peter was one of her regular customers in Woolworth's. He followed her around the shop and bought small items from whatever section she happened to be in charge of at the time. The other girls had noticed Peter watching Sheena in the shop. She had noticed him herself.

'Oh, here's *your* man', they'd say when he arrived through the doors, his eyes roving to find her long hair and sturdy body. She had been aware of him early on, attracted to his dark beard and neat clothes, but she didn't really speak to him until she ended up working in the children's department.

'You've bought CDs from me and Pick 'n' Mix sweeties and a non-stick pan, among other things. Are you going to buy wee kiddie's clothes from me now?' she teased. 'Or are you going to ask me out?'

Peter laughed. 'That's not a local accent', he said.

Rain scudded along Shore Street and the wind lifted everything before it. Paper and bits of seaweed slung themselves at Peter's legs as he made his way towards The Highlander. An orchestra of ropes slapped in a frenzy against the flagpoles along the pier and somewhere a bell tinkled. The chandlers and the gift shop were still open, plying for the last scrapings of tourist business. The light from their windows threw long golden streaks onto the soaking roadway. He pulled his jacket over his head, not wanting the rain to slide the gel from his hair and make it land in fragrant drips on his collar.

The Highlander was wedged with people when he got there. The wood-panelled walls warmed the place as much as the huddle of people. Pool balls cracked across a table in the corner and music hummed from speakers set into the ceiling. Peter didn't know many people, but he saw Alasdair wave at him from the bar and went to join him. He spotted the girl from the bakery. She was wearing a sleeveless T-shirt and her breasts pushed against the material in two large mounds. He felt a rush between his legs as he walked past her to the bar.

'There you are, Peter', said Alasdair, 'what can I get you?'

'I'll have a lager, thanks'.

He took the foaming pint and followed Alasdair to where the rest of the party was sitting. He greeted Alasdair's wife and found himself beside John, the postman. He accepted John's offer of a Marlboro, though he'd been off cigarettes for a while. He didn't like the way they made his breath smell.

'How long have you been in Strathross now, Peter?' asked John.

'About two months, I suppose'.

'And what brings you so far north?'

'Oh, the good clean air', laughed Peter, dragging on his cigarette.

'You're here two months, you say. It's time we found you a lassie, isn't that right Alasdair?' said John.

'Maybe it's not girls he likes at all, eh Peter?' Alasdair grinned, winking at him.

'Oh, I have a lassie', said Peter.

'Oh, aye', said John, looking around, 'so where is she?'

'In Glasgow', he replied, pulling at his beard.

'Glasgow? She's not much use to you there, son. So what's her name, this girl?'

'Her name's Sheena. Sheena McLeod'.

'Oh, a good Highland name', said John, clinking his glass off Peter's and slapping him on the shoulder.

'Oh, aye', said Peter, taking a long drink from his pint that left a white froth over his moustache. He jumped up off the seat and wove through the crowd to the bar to get in a round of drinks. After ordering, he turned to look out over the smoky room and noticed the girl from the bakery coming towards him. She slid in beside him at the counter and pressed the side of her body against him. Her dark eyes lifted to his.

'It's packed in here, isn't it?' she said.

'It is'.

He nodded at her and scooped the three pints he had ordered into his hands. He steered his way back to his seat, trying not to slosh the beer over the sides of the glasses.

'That's a lovely girl', said John, cupping his two hands in front of his chest and tittering into Peter's face. Peter smiled at him and finished his old pint to make way for the new.

The outside of the funeral parlour off Sauchiehall Street was as decorative as a lady's fashion boutique. 'McKay's Funeral Directors, Glasgow' twirled its way across the shiny black sign in heavy silver letters. The large front windows were hung with burgundy velvet drapes.

McKay was fastidious; a good teacher. He let Peter help him with all of the work in hand even though he had no experience at all.

'You won't learn anything just by watching, you have to do the things yourself to get a feel for them', he said.

McKay was of full of opinions. One of them was that a good embalming service was what made a successful funeral home. He told Peter several times that he had personally attended cosmetic and hairdressing courses and that he wasn't afraid to discuss their merits. No, not at all.

'A well embalmed remains is like a parting gift to a family', he told Peter. 'It's not acceptable to present the deceased to their loved ones in a slipshod way. It's your job as a Restorative Artist to make the remains look as happy and healthy as they did in life. We don't want any nasty sights upsetting the families, after all. Now, do we?'

Peter filled a notebook with everything that McKay taught him. After work each evening he would buy a few cans of beer and sprawl in his bed-sit, scribbling onto the pages everything he remembered from that day. He categorised what McKay taught him under different headings:

Embalming Fluids: The fluids injected into the deceased serve to protect the living from infection. There are dyes in the embalming fluids that help to restore the natural skin colour.

Cosmetology: This is an important part of the embalmer's work, as is hairdressing. Badly styled hair can be most upsetting to the family of the deceased.

With skill, a good embalmer can help to avoid a Closed Coffin funeral from occurring.

McKay switched on the Porti-Boy and began to prepare the body of an old woman for embalming. The stainless steel machine glinted under the white light.

'Car smash', he said, looking over at Peter. 'Imagine getting to that age and being killed in a bloody car crash. It's shocking. The poor wee woman'.

The woman's skull was crushed and bruises raged across her forehead. Peter moved closer and touched her tiny hand. It was cold and hard. He thought she looked calm and peaceful, despite her injuries.

McKay showed him how to inject the sterilising fluids into the body. He placed his hands over Peter's to guide him.

'These go into the circulatory system to preserve and disinfect the corpse. They also restore the skin's colour'. McKay liked to talk as he worked, explaining the methods over and over to be sure that Peter understood. 'You can get a very natural looking skin tone with the new embalming fluids that are on the market. Even still, sometimes the skin can look a bit waxy, almost like lard', he explained. 'But that's nothing a bit of rouge won't sort out'.

McKay worked away, getting Peter to stand close and letting him operate the machine and examine the results of their work. The wan pallor fell from the old woman's cheeks and Peter stared as she seemed to be flushed with life.

'Now look at her', said McKay, with satisfaction. 'Any man's fancy'.

Sheena grinned at him and he smiled back. She stood up and the sun hung behind her so that he couldn't see her face. She flipped her long plait back with a swing of her neck and pulled the straps of her top down off her shoulders, swaying her hips to an imaginary song. Peter groaned and lunged at her. They laughed and kissed and rolled around on the grass. He pulled her head back with her hair and she yelped.

'Stop it, you're hurting me!' He pulled again, wrapping the plait around his hand so that his fist was close to the back of her neck. He kissed her hard on the mouth but she pulled away.

'Stop it, Peter, let go'. Her face was flushed and she pushed him off her when he unwound his hand from her hair. 'You're crazy'.

'Touchy', he sneered.

'I've got to get back to work'.

Sheena stood, grabbed her bag and walked away. She didn't look back at him. I'll show her a thing or two tonight, he thought, lying back in the grass and squinting at the sun.

The house on Argyll Street was dark. Peter's legs wobbled as he stood in front of the door and tried to get the key into the lock. Drops from the gutter splashed into his eyes and he staggered backwards to shake his fist at the sky. He finally managed to get the key to meet the lock and he lurched into the house, fumbling for the light switch in the hall. The smell that clung to everything made him gasp.

'Jesus', he moaned, covering his face with his hand.

He went into the kitchen and took a long piss into the sink, grunting when he'd finished. Then he launched down the corridor to the bedroom and turned on the light. The butterfly over by the window fluttered and Peter turned to see where the noise was coming from. He thought that someone might be looking in through the window, that there might be a gap in the curtains. He pulled at the curtains and the butterfly scattered along the windowsill. He grabbed at it, caught it by the wings and lifted it close to his face to look at it. Its feelers wagged and waved. He crushed it between his finger and thumb, then stared at the powdery mess it had left behind and laughed.

He fell onto the bed beside Sheena and lifted the heavy plait of her hair and laid it carefully across her neck. He had noticed that the marks around her throat were beginning to show through again. He smoothed the folds of her dress and put his arm across her body.

'I don't like that postman', he slurred. 'That John. John the postman. Do you? He's rude. He's a rude fucker. But Alasdair's alright and his wife. And that wee Australian girl with the red hair. She's nice. You know the new one from the bakery? She's lovely. A lovely girl'. His words tumbled out in slow motion; he was starting to fade away into sleep. 'The light's still on', he mumbled. 'The light's on, Sheena. Be a pet and turn it off'. He pucked her in the side. '*Go* on, love, turn off the light', he whispered.

But Sheena didn't move. Peter fell asleep and the rasp of his snores echoed around the room as he lay beside her on the bed. His chest bellowed up and down and a line of spit dribbled from his mouth onto the pillow. The dull bulb that hung in the centre of the ceiling gave off a depressing light and Sheena's ashy skin gleamed. Peter slept, his arm still thrown around her waist and she lay there beside him on her back. Keeping very still.

ANYTHING STRANGE OR STARTLING?

My Ma has used up all the juice again. Last week I asked could she get two cartons of orange from now on because there was never any for me and Liam. She went mad, shouting so much that frothy bits appeared at the sides of her mouth; it reminded me of the scurf that floats on the top of the river. Liam calls that Guinness water.

'Do you think I'm Rockefeller?' she roared. 'Do I think I'm Rothschild?' She lost the cool with me for ten minutes.

'OK, OK, I was only saying', I said, and she called me a cheeky pup and said to get out of her sight.

There's no juice left because Ma knocked it back with her drink. That means I have to get Liam ready for school and he'll keep saying 'I want Mammy'. I like a drop of orange in the mornings. Even though it makes my throat creamy, it's quite refreshing. It goes well with toast and marmalade. I don't drink tea anymore. I gave it up when I was eight. First of all I gave up sugar in my tea, but eventually I gave up tea altogether. I think I feel better for it. Ma loves a nice cup of tea. She likes it strong; strong enough to dry her mouth. 'Weak tea is piss water', she says, but not in front of visitors, only to us and to her friend, Mona.

Mona has hands that are knotted like birdclaws, but Ma doesn't mind – she thinks Mona is a marvel. She calls her a girl even though she must be about fifty. Mona's husband,

Noel, is a lousy eejit. He has a preggy belly and sideburns like sweeping brushes. The state of him, Ma says, and Mona laughs, but then sometimes she doesn't laugh. Sometimes she's in love with Noel.

Me and Liam play 'Mona'; we pick up our cups of milk with claw hands and say 'Indeed and it is' and 'Indeed and it does' and 'Anything strange or startling?' That's the way Mona goes on. Ma caught us at it before. 'Stop that, you brats', she said, but she laughed.

I make a cup of tea for Ma and bring it to her room. It smells like dirty tights and talc in there in the mornings and the air is always warm. Her head sticks out of the sheets and her cheeks are pink. Her pink cheeks are called grog blossoms and she only gets them when she's after having a drink. She covers them with foundation if she has to go anywhere. She is so pale the rest of the time that I like her grog blossoms; they make her look happy. She was crying again last night.

'A cup of tea', I whisper, and she pulls herself up groaning.

'Leave it there, like a good girl', she says, pointing at the bedside table. She squeezes my hand and tries to give me a kiss, but I have to turn my head because of the sour smell. She drops my hand and pushes me away.

'Go on so, Little Miss Prim', she says. That's what she calls me.

I get Liam's breakfast ready and then I pull him out of bed. His hair is all over the place so I brush it down while he eats. I do my own hair then and leave the hairbrush back on the counter for Ma. I have to clean out Liam's lunchbox before I can put the lunch in. This delays us. Then I'm late for meeting Marie and she will walk on without me. Marie is my best friend on earth. She is Welsh, from Wales, and soon, she says, she is leaving this kip to go back there. I hope she never goes.

Sure enough she is gone on ahead by the time I get down past the river and I just hope that she hasn't walked to school with Anne. Anne is always trying to steal Marie away. I'd love to give that Anne a good box in the stomach or a bite on the cheek or something like that. She has fat lips and blonde hair because her family is rich. She wears a red kilt with a pin on it and I would like one of them. I wish bad things would happen to her, but then sometimes I feel remorse because Granny used to say that in the eyes of God thinking a bad thing is as bad as doing it. But I'm not sure if I believe that. Anyway, since Granny died I don't have to go to Mass anymore. Ma says that the priests have too much old blether. Mass is boring and everyone only sits there with their minds wandering, pretending to be holy.

At school, before the teacher comes in, they're all on about the volcano that erupted. It's Mount St Helens this and Mount St Helens that, as if any of them had ever been there. Still, I get swept away and next thing I know I'm saying that my uncle lives in Washington in a big wooden house. They're all looking at me.

'Yes', I say, 'he saw the whole thing. The volcano erupted, the smoke blotted out the sun and molten lava shot right past his door, killing dogs and people and everything'.

'How do you know?' says Anne.

'Because he rang us right when it was happening', I say.

'I didn't know youse had a phone', she says, real sly.

'They just got one in', says Marie, saving your neck.

That Anne is a greasy cow, I hate her flabby mouth.

On the way home Marie asks if I really have an uncle in Washington and I say yes, keeping up the lie, even though she's my best friend. My face is going red, so I tell her about the date that Ma had on Saturday night.

'They went to the pictures to see *The Elephant Man*. Ma said that it was morbid and she nearly fell asleep. She said "What kind of a gobshite brings a woman to see a film like that?"'

Marie laughs. 'A big gobshite', she says. Then she tells me that she's going away, her and her family. 'Back to Cardiff, out of this hole at last'.

I can't believe it; she seems so happy. I shuffle along beside her.

'We're going away too', I say, after a minute. She asks where we are going. 'We're going to Washington, if you must know', I say, very loud.

She looks at me sideways. Then I run off home because I think I'm going to cry. The front door is locked and it's Mona who answers it.

'There you are', she says, her hook hands curved into her chest, 'anything strange or startling?' Her voice is funny and she's looking over my head, instead of at my face. I go into the kitchen and ask where my Ma is.

'Ah, now', says Mona, still not looking at me, 'she's had to take a little trip for herself. Noel and me are going to mind the two of you until she's able to get back'.

Liam is at the table. Noel is sitting in Ma's chair, scoffing chips.

'There you are, love', he grunts, 'have your dinner now'.

I can see all the mashed up chips through his teeth.

'I'm not your love', I say and go into my room.

Ma looks as pale as paper when we go to visit her. She's wearing a hospital nightdress and it rustles when she moves. There is a smell in the ward like clean on top of dirty and the women in the beds stare at us when Mona brings us in. One of them calls us over, but she's talking gibberish and we can't understand a word. Liam giggles.

Ma's eyes are puffed up and red. Her arms lie flopped in front of her. They are in bits, covered in brown trails of scabs that have high pink sides. Liam puts his finger on the cuts. She touches his cheek and he starts to cry.

'There now, Little Pudding', she says, but she is nearly crying too. She takes the flowers we've brought and sniffs them but they are chrysanthemums and they have no real smell. 'They're gorgeous, kids, thanks', says Ma, very quietly.

'Indeed and they are', says Mona and pats Liam on the head with her crabby hand. He pulls his head away from her, tossing his hair.

Ma has nothing to say for herself and it's hard to know what to say to her. Mona tells her that the death toll from the volcano has reached fifty-eight and that Noel is gone in to have his corns pared. Ma doesn't say anything, she just stares. It's like as if she's asleep but awake at the same time. I tell her that Marie and her family are going back to Wales. She nods. I want her to say something but she is miles away.

'This place is stinky', says Liam, 'it smells like bums'.

I give him a puck to shut him up but Ma laughs.

'You're right, you know', she says, and we all laugh, but Mona laughs a bit too hard.

'It's not *that* funny', I say and she stops.

'I'll just go and ask the nurse for a vase for the flowers', says Mona.

'Well', whispers Ma to us.

'Well', Liam says, 'what happened to your arms?'

'I had an accident. I was attacked by a lawnmower'. She smiles.

Liam stares at her all gawpy-eyed. 'Noel won't let us watch what we want to on the telly', he says.

'When are you getting out?' I ask.

'I'll be out next week and we'll go to the zoo, just the three of us'.

The last time you all went to the zoo she met a chap, and you ended up in a pub on Parkgate Street for the rest of the day, with her doing false laughs and him grabbing at her. Afterwards she called him a mean little scut because he didn't give us a lift home.

'Not the zoo', I say.

She moves in the bed and reaches over to her locker but she can't pull the door open. 'I've a few sweets in here'. The paper nightdress makes scratchy noises. It has no back and her grey bra strap is on view. I rush to help her open the drawer so that she'll sit back in the bed and not be making a show of us all. She is still stretching. 'Oh feck', she yelps, holding onto her arm. One of her cuts has opened and big globs of blood are sliding down her wrist onto the bedspread.

Mona comes hurtling down the ward and then runs off screaming 'Nurse, Nurse' as if someone is choking to death. The nurse says it would be best if Ma rested, cutting short our visit. Mona pushes us out of the place, hardly giving us a chance to say goodbye. All the loonies start waving, thinking we've been in to visit them.

'The poor creatures', says Mona, too loud.

Liam is lashing a football at the front wall when I get home from school. Ma is buckled again, sitting at the table with a bottle.

'I thought you weren't supposed to drink with those tablets', I say.

'You', she slurs at me, 'you're the cause of it all'.

I hate when she's like this.

'Go to bed, Ma, and give me that bottle'.

She jumps up and lunges at me.

'Get off my lip', she screams into my face, grabbing at my clothes.

I run into my room and lock the door. I lie on the bed thinking of the volcano in Washington, thinking that it might be easier to live there than here, until I fall asleep. When I wake up again it's already dark and the house is quiet.

PEACE BE WITH YOU, PHILOMENA

Philomena was sick of pulling her husband up off the floor, dragging him up and feeding his head into the toilet. It was bad enough that he came home pissed, she was fecked if she was going to spend every night of her life mopping up his puke, her head reeling.

But on those nights, once she had removed her hands from his body and shaken off the feeling of him, she could say anything to him. She would stand over him with her hands on her hips and her elbows pointed out from her body like wings.

'Come on, Martin, you big eejit, stick your head down that jax and get it all up. You're worse than any baby, do you know that? At least babies grow up. Jesus, what did you eat, you greedy pig? Come on! Wipe that slop off your chin'.

She would swipe at him with a rolled up magazine and slap his cheeks with it. Martin's head would loll and his eyeballs would sling around inside their sockets like jellied marbles. He groaned and hiccupped and wagged his finger at her to make a point. But the words wouldn't form themselves. Philomena would stand over his slumpy body and laugh, delighted with the freedom of being herself.

On the nights she couldn't move him, she left him in the bathroom, his face sliding in a slick of bile, and went back to bed. She hoped he would stay there all night, sprawled on the tiles, snoring and pissing himself. He probably has toilet dreams, she thought, and him lying there in the shadow of the pot. He wouldn't remember anything the next day. Or if he did, he never said.

Philomena was only skin on bones; she kept herself small to be out of everyone's way. It made her life easier. She had a secret, an unusual gift, and because of it she feared the touch of other people's skin. Because just by brushing off another person's hand, or any bare part of their body, Philomena felt as if she was inside them. She became swallowed up in the other person's skin.

Wheeling her shopping trolley around Dunnes Stores she would pull herself in, melding her elbows tight to her sides, making sure not to tip off the people beside her. Touching others meant sliding inside their skin, knowing their body and its clumsiness. It meant she knew their desires; she felt the fuzz of their hairy places and the push of their secret pimples. The feeling only ever lasted for a few minutes but it made her feel nude, uncomfortable.

But in the night, when Martin hauled himself on top of her and grabbed between her legs, she fell into some place that didn't belong to either of them. The slap of his clammy skin against her own pushed her far back into her mind. A sort of drunkenness wound itself around her and she cowered in that place until the heaving stopped and Martin rolled off, pulling a damp trail behind him. It was better that way.

She had told her mother once, about knowing what it felt like to wear another person's skin. Bridie was slapping pastry dough across the table making lids for rhubarb tarts and Philomena was helping her. She was sprinkling sugar in drifts across the sour stalks of fruit that sat in baking tins all around the kitchen. She wouldn't have said anything, only she thought that it was something everybody knew.

'Daddy has a hard place. It makes him feel warm', she said.

Her mother stopped and stared at her and then she thumped her hard on the arm. The sugar Philomena was spooning scattered across the table.

'What are you saying?' roared Bridie. 'Has he *touched* you?' She emphasised the word so that her daughter would know she was referring to a certain kind of touching.

'Yes', answered Philomena, meaning only that her father had squeezed her hand or slapped at her bum when she passed by him as she skipped through the house.

Her mother sat all day at the kitchen table waiting for her husband to come home. She twisted her apron around her hands and the uncooked pastry sat in yellowing mounds on the table, the fat at its core going rancid. Philomena hung by the cooker, singing sad songs inside her head. Bridie stood abruptly when her husband came through the door and her chair reeled and clattered onto the floor behind her.

'Bridie, what's wrong? Is somebody dead?'

'Did you *touch* her?' she whispered tautly.

'What?' He stared from Philomena to her mother.

'Did you *touch* her, Jim?' she shouted, pointing at their daughter.

'I did no such thing!' he roared back. 'No such thing!'

Philomena shied back against the wall, hoping that he'd use the stick to beat her, rather than his hand, so that she wouldn't have to feel the warmth from his hard place come through him to her.

She was born in 1961, the year the martyr she was named for was removed from the calendar of saints. Bones and blood and a few small miracles weren't enough to keep a soul saintly forever, it seemed. But the people of St Philomena's parish, where Bridie and Jim lived, were not willing to let go of their saint.

'What about her miraculous recovery after the flogging?' they muttered to each other after Mass each Sunday, when they congregated in front of the church doors.

'And what about the arrows that wouldn't pierce her skin when they tried to kill her? How do they explain *that?*'

No, they would not lose their saint and, in an act of rebellious loyalty, most of the baby girls born in the parish that year were named Philomena.

'Now', said Bridie with satisfaction, after her daughter's christening. 'Philomena Frances. Meaning *Beloved* and *Free*'.

After making the mistake of telling her mother about her gift, Philomena chose to hide it. She never talked about the time she spent occupying other people's bodies, feeling their sweat leaking through pores as if it were her own, knowing the rattle of their breath. She told no one else a thing about it, not even Martin when she loved him first.

When Philomena's friend, Catherine, turned forty, her husband, Brendan, brought her to Paris for a treat. She came back glowing, full of love for the man who knew how to treat a wife. Philomena knew that no such thing could be expected of Martin. August and her fortieth birthday rolled nearer and she waded deeper into herself.

On a rainy July afternoon she went to meet Catherine for tea in Bewley's on Grafton Street, her favourite coffee house. She was relieved to get a seat to herself on the bus and she breathed deep on the beautiful hoppy smell that fingered its way over the quays from the James' Gate brewery. In the café she took the chair opposite her friend and squeezed her hand across the table.

'Tell me all about Paris, Cath', she said.

Gripping her friend's fingers inside her own she felt the heat in her belly and the rush to her breasts while Catherine described her trip.

'Oh, Phil, you'd love it! It's exactly what you'd expect, all old buildings, wide streets and beautiful people. We ate in bistros, mostly, drinking little *pichets* of red wine and trying food we'd never heard of. We were like honeymooners, for God's sake! And the French are so nice. We didn't meet any of those rude Parisians you always hear about. We went to the Marché aux Puces at St Ouen and Bren haggled for ages to buy me an antique bracelet. It's absolutely gorgeous, I'll show it to you when you come over'.

At home that evening Philomena was mulish with Martin, handing him an excuse to go to the pub.

'I don't know why you bother with that Catherine. You're always in a foul mood after you meet her'.

'Maybe it's coming back to you that puts me in bad form', she snapped.

'Well, I'm not sitting here looking at your miserable face for the night'.

No, but I'll have to look at yours, puking your ring up later on, won't I? she thought, watching him head for the front door.

After he left, she wandered through the house, touching things. She flicked the television on and off, then tried to read some poetry. She kept thinking about Catherine's trip to Paris and how different things might be if only Martin didn't drink so much. He wasn't bad, really, he just needed to ease off on the pub. She found it impossible to settle to anything so she decided to clear out some of the boxes in the spare room.

They never used the room and when she opened the door she got a peculiar smell, like smouldering ashes or old leaves. She sat on her hunkers in the middle of the floor, hauling boxes towards her to see what was in them and what she might be able to get rid of. Most of it was hers. All of her childhood stuff that her mother had cleared out as soon as she had left home, as if she couldn't bear to hold onto any sign of her. It's only taken me ten years to get around to unpacking it, Philomena thought.

Her college books were there and her collection of foreign dolls, their hair and skirts clotted with years of dust, each one a present from holidays that didn't include her. She found old hit singles and her art portfolio from secondary school. She looked through the charcoal portraits she had done of her classmates and laughed at their wonky teenage features. Catherine was there, her school-tie in a neat knot at her throat, twenty-five years less of living on her face.

Dusk had settled and the room was nearly dark. Philomena changed her position on the floor and felt dizzy from sitting with her legs tucked under her for so long. The smoky smell she had noticed earlier seemed to be getting stronger. It was a sweet smell that reminded her of incense wafted from a church censer, or the smoke that comes from the resin on burning logs.

What *is* that? she wondered. She hopped up and turned on the light and saw curls of smoke coming from under the table in the comer. She looked underneath it and saw that the smoke was rising from a cardboard box with the logo Flahavan's Progress Oatlets bannered in red on its side. The box had been shoved far in under the table.

'What the hell ...?' said Philomena, pulling the box out and flicking back the lid.

Inside, tucked into wads of newspapers, was a statue of a girl with long dark hair. A scarlet cloak sat in rigid folds over her virgin blue tunic and she had a crown of roses wound around her head. In her hands she carried two arrows and a palm branch. Tiny wisps of smoke seemed to blow all around her and then disappear.

She stared at the plaster figure for a few moments. It was the statue of Saint Philomena that her father had given her as a Confirmation present. He had carried it in his lap on the aeroplane, all the way back from the parish pilgrimage to Rome.

'There you are', he had said, handing it to her, 'a lovely statue for a lovely girl. One Philomena for another'.

'There you are', breathed Philomena, lifting the statue from its bed of newspapers and touching the saint's face, which was the colour of a hen's egg.

'And there you are', said a pure, light voice. 'Long time no see'.

Philomena whipped her head around and nearly let the statue fall from her hands. She looked quickly over at the closed door and then stared around the room.

'Who spoke?' she whispered.

'I did. I spoke. Me!'

Philomena stared at the statue she was holding. The fuchsia painted lips were still but the voice sounded clearly again. 'Hello, hello! Remember me?'

Philomena peered at the statue. She held it up to the light and examined the sweet plaster features, squinting as she looked into its tiny eyes.

'You've got to be joking', she said.

Paris suited her. She spent her first day following the trail of the artists she loved, up rue Lepic with its streaming cobbles, to the Butte and all around the laneways of Montmartre. She ate in *Au Grain de Folie*, marvelling at the efficiency of the woman who took her order, cooked her food and served it in a flurry of good manners. She thought that Martin would hate the little café with its shabby place mats and exposed kitchen, and that made her smile and enjoy it all the more.

On the Saturday she drank several *pichets* of Bordeaux at a pavement café and watched all the comings and goings on the Boulevard St Michel. She bought Moroccan tea glasses at a street market and some Provencal lavender to slip under her pillow. Maybe it will help me to sleep through Martin's drunken homecomings in future, she thought.

That night, in her hotel room, she watched Marlon Brando *rrrr*oll his *rrrr*'s in a French version of *The Godfather*. The statue of her namesake sat on top of the TV, smiling her approval, the light from the screen fluttering across her benevolent face.

On her last day in Paris, Philomena crossed the river to the Musée d'Orsay and stood in front of Manet's *Olympia*, crying at the painting's perfect beauty. Her small body rattled and she swiped at her tears, annoyed with herself. She sat a long time in the café behind the clock flicking through the postcards and books she had bought in the gallery's shop, lingering over *Olympia's* perfect skin and assured gaze. Why can't I be serene and powerful like you? she thought with a sigh.

Back out in the open air she leafed through the bookstalls on the *quais* beside the pea-green river and bought a vintage copy of *Playboy* for Martin. That'll give him a thrill, she thought. The silly shite.

Ryanair wafted her towards home that evening and Philomena lounged in her window seat, sipping a glass of red wine and singing a wild version of 'Happy Birthday to Me' in her head. Up over the Cliffs of Dover she flew, thinking how much they looked like enormous teeth biting their way across the channel to Brittany. She stared down at London scattered below the aeroplane, the Thames sneaking its way through the city in silence.

And she thought a lot about how things were going to be with Martin, how she was going to tell him a thing or two about himself and about herself, and about how their lives were going to go on from here. By God things are going to change, thought Philomena, draining her wine glass, and I am going to have peace.

She settled down into her seat feeling the warmth of the wine in her neck. She closed her eyes, dropped her head back and smiled.

'Peace be with you, Philomena', she murmured, 'and a very happy birthday to you, too'.

BABIES MERRY

Tess sometimes still woke in the night with a claggy tongue and two crescents of sweat spreading under her breasts like mildew. For a while she would believe that her head was muzzy from drink and that she could hear a child crying in the room across the landing. Then slowly she would let in the heaving wind and the slap of the waves on the strand and she'd realise where she was. Tonight she had been dreaming and had woken with a kick. She had realised lately that her dreams were always set firmly in the past and she wondered why that should be.

She padded down the stairs. At the back door she pulled on, over her nightdress, the overcoat that they shared and she slipped into her rubber boots. Betty mooched in her basket in the kitchen and Tess whispered 'Good dog, good girl' so that she'd stay where she was. The cotton bed-socks she wore made the boots feel damp and big on her feet. She left the house, being careful to go quietly so as not to waken Kay, who needed more sleep than most.

It was nearly dawn and a flap of light was lifting over the sea. Tess had the beach all to herself and the scrunch of the washy pebbles under her boots was comforting, a sure thing. She scooped into her hands a mix of withered shells and stones the colour of boiled lobster, studying them for a while, before scattering them back at her feet. She strode by the shoreline, the wind pulling at her legs, and kicked at the bladderwrack that was heaped on the sand. The pods stuck to it looked like clusters of tiny frogs. On warm days black flies clung to the seaweed and rose lazily when she swiped at it, but there were no flies tonight.

She watched a line of seagulls follow each other along the shore like sheep and then bent to collect a few more scallop shells for the garden, shoving them into the pockets of the coat. Tess sucked in the wet, fishy smells of the sea and wondered when she'd ever get used to living here again.

Kay was sitting at the kitchen table, drinking tea, when she got back. Her grey hair was trapped into pink sponge rollers, and the lines of her scalp shone through in the light.

'Morning', she said, not looking around.

'You're up', replied Tess.

Kay had left Tess's green mug on the counter, a drop of milk in the bottom of it. She made the tea the way their mother always had, milk first. Tess preferred to do it the other way, to add the milk after the tea was poured, but she never said anything. The toast popped and Kay got up and placed a slice on a plate and put it in front of her. Tess took the toast off the plate and propped it against the marmalade jar.

'You know I hate that', she said, 'the plate gets sweaty and it makes the toast go all chewy'. She was sorry the second she had said it, but Kay just rolled her eyes.

'You're such a fussy fecker', she said.

'And you, my dear, are as calm as a cow'.

'Oh, charming, that's exactly what I want to be called first thing in the morning – a cow!'

They both laughed and Tess thought that it might be a good day.

The house smelt the way it always had, smooth like butchers' paper or fresh paint, but it was never as clean now as it had been in their mother's day. Kay hadn't changed anything, the same over-flowered curtains and wallpaper still loomed in every room and the same pictures had survived on each wall. On the mantelpiece sat the photo of their father holding a large fish. His hair was parted far to one side and it sat in waves; a cigarette hung from his smile. Their mother's picture was austere and formal compared to his; her square face held shy eyes. There was a familiarity to everything that made Tess uneasy. Half of the time she expected her mother to bluster through the front door, undoing her headscarf and saying that there was a shocking storm forecast, had they heard it on the wireless?

Tess spent the morning out the back, weeding. Kay wasn't much of a gardener, so there was plenty to do. She wondered if Barry would ring again, he had said that he would. Their first conversation had been painful, drowned in silence. She drove the hoe into the edges of the pathway and turned out the weeds and soil. The earth was peat-black and rich with worms. Kay came down the garden to her, Betty dragging along behind, panting.

'That dog is on the way out', Tess said.

'Do you want tea?' asked Kay, glancing down at Betty. 'Aren't the daffodils gorgeous?'

'Ah, no, I'll finish this first'.

'I'm thinking of going up to do the grave tomorrow. Do you want to come?'

'I will, so', said Tess, even though every graveyard she had ever been in made her feel bad, as if the grief of each mourner had settled around the gravestones.

'Barry rang'.

Tess stopped working. 'What? Why didn't you call me?'

'He said not to. He said he'll come with the child on Sunday, if that suits. I said it'd suit fine'.

'But ...' She didn't finish, she stared at her sister. 'It is fine, I suppose'.

It lashed rain all that night. Tess found it hard to sleep; she could hear the raindrops hopping off the window and the hard mattress was clinging to her bones every time she woke up. She moved her hands down over her hips, pulling at the loose skin of her stomach, and swung her legs around inside the bed meeting cold spots on the sheets. She wondered what he'd think of her, this child, this small part of her that she'd never met. And what would Barry be like after all these years; would he still be the image of his father, or would he be a little bit more like the Merrys now, like her side? Funny how even a young baby could look so much like an adult, she thought. He wouldn't remember anything about her, but would he have forgiven her? Could he ever forgive her?

The rain made the sea push and rage and the wind screeched around every window in the house. Tess longed for sleep but her head was crowded with thoughts of their father. His sister, their auntie Kathleen, had told them how delighted he had been when they were born. His twin baby girls. He wondered if he was seeing double, Kathleen had said. He was so thrilled with them that he had taken the boat out on a bad morning, only days after they were born, to share the happy news with his friend on the island. Tess remembered the way Kathleen had cried when she'd told her and Kay that he hàd ever been seen again. She told how the sea had swallowed him up and never spat him back out.

When they were very young Tess and Kay used to think that their father would come back someday. They used to say that he'd banged his head falling out of the boat and that he had floated for a while before being plucked from the sea by a whaling boat. They would lie awake at night discussing the details. Kay decided that he couldn't remember who he was and that he was brought far away over the Atlantic to Nantucket Island, somewhere off the coast of America. But one day his head would get right, Tess would say, and he'd come home to his wife and daughters and everything would be perfect. The older they got the less they talked about him coming home, until the day came that they never really talked about it again.

The grave was tucked back by the cemetery wall in the shade of an enormous yew. Their parents had bought the plot as soon as they were married. That was how it was. Tess waded through the wet grass, enjoying the cool air that lapped at her cheeks. She was always struck by the simplicity of the grey marble headstone with its white lettering: 'To the memory of Thomas Merry, lost at sea'. Their mother's inscription was bigger, carved a lifetime later. There were curls of shell and a scatter of white gravel glinting in the low-walled space in front of the headstone. A Christmas wreath lay propped against it, its red ribbon faded to pink by sun and rain.

'I wonder what he's like; Barry's son', said Tess, looking around at the other headstones. There was a traveller's grave nearby. It was huge and the face of the man who'd died was etched into the marble, a portrait from a photograph probably. Brass horses pulled carts across the grass in front of the grave and it was flanked by two luminous Blessed Virgins. Crocuses and snowdrops grew all around the edges. 'That's some grave', she said.

Kay had removed the holly wreath and was raking at the stones and shells on their parents' grave. 'It's hard to know, I suppose. I mean, what's Barry even like now?'

Tess grunted. She wondered if that was a dig, if Kay was criticising her for having been the worst kind of mother. She knelt down beside her sister and pulled at the weeds and bits of grass that were poking through the shells and stones. She could feel the damp seeping through the knees of her trousers.

'What if they don't like me?'

'Just meet them first', said Kay softly.

Though she had given up going years before, Tess went to Mass with Kay on Sunday morning. The church smelt as it had when they were growing up, warm with polish and candle wax and incense. Their neighbours nodded at them. She sat on the narrow pew and fingered the varnished back of the seat in front, glancing around at the people who sat nearby. Why can't I be more like them? she wondered. What happened to me?

When the Mass began, her responses were automatic, though she would have said that she had forgotten how to pray years ago. Still, she felt awkward, like an intruder, and she decided not to receive communion. But after the priest had chanted the Our Father, she found Kay at her back shoving her out of the pew. Tess could feel her neck getting hot.

'We'll get a cake', said Kay, as they strolled back towards the village from the church.

'Kids never like cake. Better to get biscuits, I think'.

'We *always* liked cake'.

'We had no choice', snapped Tess.

They had always been the bone and sinew of their mother's life. She put everything into them once she knew that her husband wouldn't be coming back. Kay, being the easier of the two, was her pet. Kay the obliging; Kay the smiling; Kay who gave up a life of her own to be Mam's companion. Her sister, awkward in her own skin, had found another way. Tess grew out of the house by the sea quickly; she escaped, got herself a job and a husband, and made a new life many miles away from her mother and sister.

Tess cooked a roast chicken lunch. Kay liked plain food and she kept to their mother's tradition of an early meal at the weekend.

'I'd love a drop of wine', said Tess when they had finished eating.

'Is that a good idea?'

'Probably not, no', sighed Tess. She hung by the window, fussing with the curtains, waiting for them to arrive. 'Jesus, what's keeping them?'

'Language', warned Kay, who was sitting in her armchair, eyes closed, head thrown back, enjoying the digestion of her meal. 'They'll be here any minute'.

She looked over at Kay, a little surprised as usual to see the grey-locked, podgy woman who was her twin. Past middle-age already, she thought. How can I even be this old when inside I'm the same as I ever was?

Tess didn't feel like a mother anymore. It hadn't suited her in the first place, she knew. She could never identify with the sweaty, urgent demands of Barry as a baby, or her own milky, rage-fuelled body. She regularly slipped away from him, left him with anyone who'd have him, so that her head could find peace, her body rest. She would take a bus into town and slump on a park bench trying to get over the fear and exhaustion that strangled her when she was in charge of the baby. She couldn't believe that this was what motherhood was made up of: hours of wiping, crying, holding, rocking, feeding, washing; pain and tiredness, tiredness, tiredness. The last time she left she never went back, and she was still surprised at how little regret she felt.

A red car scrunched over the gravel in front of the house.

'They're here', said Kay cheerfully, as if she'd only seen them the day before.

Tess's head danced and she could hardly swallow. 'You let them in', she pleaded. She didn't watch them get out of the car, but hung back behind the window and tried to breathe. She could hear them in the hall, Kay chattering and Barry, with the voice of a man, answering. She heard Kay thank him for some roses he'd brought, saying that Tess had a thing for yellow roses. Kay greeted the child, told him he was a fine little man. The door swung open.

'Here we are', called Kay, launching them into the room, 'say hello to your Granny'.

Tess stepped forward, her smile pulling a tight ache across her cheeks. Barry looked like her father. She scanned his face, not meeting his eyes. He had the same sideways smile as the man in the photo, the same unruly wavy hair. His son was different; fair-haired, rounded and sturdy; a little odd-looking with his drooped-over eyes.

'Say hello to Tess, Justin', Barry said to the child. She was stung. He might have said 'Say hello to your Grandmother' at least, she thought. But she moved forward, offered her hand to the small boy. He hung by his father's side, looking up at Tess from under his eyelids. She smiled down at him. Suddenly he plunged towards her and hugged her leg, burying his face into her thigh. Tess threw her arms in the air and laughed and she swooped her grandson into her arms.

'Well hello, little man', she whispered into his toffee-coloured hair, and she kissed the plump arc of his cheek. She looked straight at Barry and mouthed a 'Thank you', and he nodded and smiled. Tess relaxed into the sofa with Justin on her lap, and Barry sat beside her and they talked.

Outside the wind gathered and lifted, pulling the spray from the sea and throwing it against the seaweedy rocks. Seagulls called and fell with the gusty air, and the sand on the shore settled and shook, shook and settled.

FINGER

When they talk about it, I notice that their voices dip lower, as if they're afraid some stranger might overhear and hold it against them. No one ever mentions it in front of my Mother, not wanting to upset her, even after all this time.

I imagine her as a baby, not slim like she is now, tired in her bones, but round and firm like a ball of bog butter. I think of her with fair hair, though really I'm not sure if she was dark or light when she was born.

I've always liked to hold her hands in mine and compare the shape of her skin with my own. My hands are pale, barely marked. Hers are bursting with ropes of veins that are the colour of faded tattoos; and freckles with blurred edges cascade over the hills of her knuckles. A ruddy knobble of flesh sits at the base of her right pinkeen, inviting my fingers to fondle it, feel its stumpiness. I ask her to tell me about that raw mound of skin as I slide my forefinger over it, thinking that because I'm an adult now, she might talk to me. Put her own words on it.

'You know well what that is', she says, and pulls both of her hands back into her lap. I withdraw, sorry that I have offended her.

Raj, my husband, has perfect hands. He doesn't realise what a large part they formed in my initial attraction to him; the huge manliness of them. They are cocoa coloured on the backs, with sprouts of coarse hairs. His fingers are long and tapered like two rows of dark candles. But it's the palms of his hands that I really love: their lightness compared to the rest of his skin; the rivers of creases like burnt earth crossing over and back across his square palms; the rough pads of his fingertips. My fascination with his hands doesn't interest him; he doesn't get it.

My Uncle Matt reckons that babies don't feel pain. But he only says that to free my Grandfather of blame, not wanting to own up to any possibility of wrongness in the family. I contradict him and say that, of course, they feel pain, that they have nerve endings the same as the rest of us.

'But they don't understand it', he says.

'But that doesn't mean that they don't feel it', I say, amazed at his thinking.

'Anyway, what's done is done', he finishes.

My Mother as a baby. Wearing her own Mother as a neck band, the midwife easing her slick body out into the world. Her Father pacing the fields, maybe, or at a neighbour's home, getting through it. The other children brought away from the house so as not to hear their Mother's roars.

The midwife bathing the baby, softly wiping her clear of grease and blood. She wraps her, first in a towel, then in a shawl and hands her over to her Mother to be fed. Both are exhausted, glad it's all over. The baby sucks, her tongue gripping the nipple expertly. My Grandfather comes back to the house.

'How is she? Is everything alright?'

'Everything's fine'.

'Thanks be to God', he says and shakes the midwife's hand, closing both of his own around hers.

'It's a fine healthy girl. Over seven pounds'.

'A girl', he says. 'Well'. He opens the door to the bedroom and his wife calls him in. She asks if he would like to hold his new daughter. The midwife waits in the doorway. He picks up the tired bundle, peers into her puckered face, admires her tiny mouth. He peels back the shawl to slot his finger into the curl of the baby's fist. 'Jesus in Heaven', he cries.

'What? What is it?' His wife pulls her sweaty head from the pillow.

'I thought you said she was alright', he says to the midwife.

'She is alright, Paddy, calm down'.

'Look at her', he says, pulling the baby's hand up to show them. There is an extra finger, a slender bud, growing from the side of her hand, right beside her smallest finger. 'She's deformed'.

'It's alright, Paddy. That's perfectly normal, it's nothing to worry about'.

He stares at the hand, gripping the baby's tiny arm between his forefinger and thumb, marking the skin. She starts to whimper, turns her head to find her Mother's breast.

'Hand her back, now', demands his wife, lifting her arms to him.

He turns away, stands for a moment before striding from the room, the baby held close to his chest. The midwife sits on the bed with the Mother, holds her hand in her own, rubs her other hand across the woman's shoulders.

They hear the yelp, the screams, the pitched wailing that won't stop. When he comes back into the room he's crying, tears coursing from his eyes onto the baby's head. His shirt is wet with blood, the baby's hand is roughly bandaged. The midwife lifts her from his arms.

'She's fixed now', he says, and walks away.

FLEECE

I woke up in the shadow of a dry-stone wall, its stones stacked as perfectly as a honeycomb. I'd fallen there in the dark, on my way back from the pub, the only place to go for miles. Even though it was summer, the cold had reeked through to my bones and I was stiff everywhere. My head had landed on a muck-clump and there were pearls of sheep shit stuck to my cheek. I picked them off and the movement of my hand made my brain lift away from my skull.

I heaved myself to sit. The air was dew-fresh and I sucked it through my nose, loving its coldness. I looked around; there was no sign of Marty. The little scut must have abandoned me and gone back to the digs by himself, I thought. He was probably horsing into the breakfast now, gearing himself up for the day's work. We had just two more sites left to survey. I wobbled to my feet and toppled forward onto the wall. The whole thing gave under me and as I pitched forward I noticed the limey coating on the stones, and how gorgeously bright it looked. I ended up face first in the next field, my cheek sliding in wet grass and my arse to the wind. I stayed there for a minute – half-laughing, half-sighing – then pulled myself up. I rebuilt the wall, stacking it up stone on stone. They were heavy and some of them slid, scraping my skin. I'd watched the farmer putting the walls back together – an ancient old fella – hauling rocks with not a bother on him, while his tractor idled and waited, like some sort of patient beast.

I was warm after building the wall and the salty wind was light and head clearing. I lit a fag and looked down over the fields. They fell away towards the sea and were empty except for the waves of mist that hovered over the grass. I pulled hard on the cigarette, letting myself choke on the lovely smoke. I thought about Marty, the screwed-up, scrunched-down state of him. He was the last person I had wanted to be sent with on an away-job; he was such a pain. I thought about thumping him in the stomach, how much I'd love it; how I should have done it in the pub when he made a fool of me, insinuating things about my mother. Marty was a thick. I hated the way he threw himself around, making me feel as small as an ant, even though I knew that I was better than him in every way. I knew it.

My mouth was clotted, woolly. I decided to head to the stream, have a drink. I dragged myself along feeling better at the thought of the clear water. I finished my fag, pinching the end and putting the butt in my pocket. It would make my jacket stink, but it was better then throwing it there for some cow or rabbit to swallow. Marty would have fecked it into the grass, still lit. He was like that. I kept my head down, stamping my feet through the damp grass, hardly lifting my eyes. Some birds swooped ahead but I didn't know what they were; they were dark-winged, round-bellied.

I heard the groan of a tractor. The ancient farmer was chugging along the boreen; his Massey Ferguson hulked under him. He stopped, leaving the engine turning over, and hopped the wall into the field I was in. He came striding towards me, the wire of his body taut and strong. I stopped and looked behind me, wondering if it was me he wanted. He came right up and stood beside me, throwing his eyes down across the fields. I wondered if he was angry with me for walking across his land. I knew that some farmers hated that, that they put up signs barring walkers of any kind. One farmer had even gone to jail over it; he threatened some hill-walkers with a gun. I'd seen him on the news.

We stood in silence, looking down over the fields. A sheep wandered up out of the mist like an apparition. It was limping, moving slow and alone across the grass. Its fleece was curled, yellow on the edges, and its face and legs were black. We watched the sheep hobble forward, its head hung low, looking like the solitary mourner at an invisible funeral. It had a wide behind; it looked sturdy apart from the dipped leg each time it limped. There were straggles of muck clinging to its underbelly.

'That's not a good sign', the farmer said. I didn't answer, not knowing exactly what he meant. Did he mean it wasn't good that the sheep was on its own because they always went around in gangs? In flocks? Or did he mean that the limping was a sign of something worse than just some sort of leg injury? I hadn't a clue about animals or the countryside or anything like that, but I didn't want to look ignorant, so I kept my mouth shut. 'You're alive anyway', he said, after a while.

'What?' I said, stupidly, looking at him, my hangover taking hold again.

'Bridie below in the B&B was worried about you. She said your friend came home last night but that you were missing. I said I'd keep an eye out'. He half-smiled at me, his face folding into lines like tree bark.

'I'm fine', I mumbled, noticing for the first time the muck that splattered my jeans. I rubbed at it, then stopped, feeling stupid and annoyed.

'You probably met a girl in the pub?' he said, smacking my shoulder. 'The girls around here are all mad for the city slickers'. He did his half-smile again and I let myself smile back; he was only poking fun.

The mist dazzled as the early morning sun rose up out of the sea. I shielded my eyes and stared at the slow dilute of the morning from pink to grey. The farmer shifted on his legs and I looked around for the lame sheep, but it was gone.

'That one's not good for much now', the farmer said and he tapped my shoulder. 'Get yourself back down to Bridie's place before she calls the police'.

I nodded and he walked away, following the path the sheep had taken. He slid through a gap in the dry-stone wall. I cut back the way I'd come and jogged to the B&B, singing as loud as I could, making up words to tunes I knew well.

On our last day before we left, Bridie came in with a black plastic sack.

'This was left for you', she said, and then she stood, waiting to see what was in it.

I opened the bag and looked in. I pulled out a sheep skin. The fleece was curled and yellow on the edges, but there were no straggles of muck. I held it up and hooted and laughed; Marty was totally pissed off, he couldn't see what was funny at all.

The Sea Saw

The sea changed the day Phoebe gave birth to Electra; it went from flat calm to a roiling mess in an hour. The water churned and roared though it had been as smooth as bone china for weeks, and it glowed green and yellow, as if lit up from the inside. Phoebe held the baby to her chest and fingered her soft-boiled cheek. She sat by the cabin's biggest window and looked down at the turning sea, wondering what presents it would have left for her on the sand. The baby slept, her fingers wound through the holes in the crocheted blanket. Phoebe heaved herself into bed, Electra still held in her arms, and breathed in her milky smell. Her dark hair settled like seaweed across the pillow. The wind burst around the cabin walls all night and waves cracked against the rocks on the shore. Morning crept up to the windows. Phoebe smiled and the baby sucked at her breast.

'Greedy little girlie', she crooned, and the baby's fist shot up, punching the air. This made her mother laugh and Electra's tiny eyelids opened to reveal navy eyes. 'Are you looking at your Mama, baby girl?'

The birth had not been hard; nearly ten months waiting had left Phoebe impatient for the pushing. She used earth-forces to get the baby out, delivering her into the water-pool like a fish. The midwife caught her, plopped her onto her mother's belly, and Electra's slippery body uncoiled under the woman's firm hands.

'Girl', she said.

'I knew', said Phoebe, cradling the baby's head to suckle while the midwife eased the afterbirth from her.

'Storm's up; I'll go when you're dressed'. The midwife towelled her down and swaddled the baby; she made tea and said she'd stop by in the morning. 'The child has health, that's the main thing; never mind that you're alone'. She moved towards the door, looked back. 'New life', she said.

Phoebe nodded.

A few days later, when a small strength flowed through her bones again, she laid Electra into a sling across her chest, took up her basket and left the cabin. She felt light, glad the low-hung weight of the baby was gone from her belly. A full moon lingered in the sky even though it was morning; Phoebe thought that its edges looked soft. She saluted the moon, hitched her baby closer in the sling, and headed down through the marram grass towards the beach. The wind sang in her ears and pulled strands of hair across her face; the salt air tasted delicious after the stuffy heat of the cabin.

She walked slowly and sang a song about lovers for Electra; the one where the woman dies and the man kisses her 'cold corpsy lips'. She made it into a lullaby. Phoebe felt full up with the wonder of her little girl, she reminded her of a kitten; the tiny face scrunched in on itself, her gaping yawns. She bent and kissed Electra's nose and the baby unpuckered, then snuggled back into her mother's breast.

The sea was still rough, its surface ploughed up like a field. There was a litter of flotsam on the strand: driftwood, net fragments, a grey bucket, several glass bottles made dull from the thrashing sea. Far off down the beach lay the carcass of a seal. Phoebe examined the pieces of driftwood, placing what she could carry into her basket. She kicked off her sandals and pushed her feet into the cold sand; it felt heavy on her toes. She lifted a cluster of mottled yellow shells and slipped the best ones into her dress pocket. They would join the rest of her collection on the windowsills; little pieces of the sea-world salvaged as ornaments.

She moved further down the beach, her eyes sweeping the debris on the sand, looking for things to take home. When she got closer to the seal she noticed that it was lying on its side; she thought she saw it move. She stood for a moment, swaying her body to keep Electra asleep. The seal's back moved again. She inched closer, unused to sharing the strand with other living things. Waves edged over her feet and she bent as she approached the animal, hoping it wasn't hurt. Phoebe began to realise that it wasn't a seal at all; it was the wrong shape. Then she stood right over where it lay and saw that it was a black-skinned man, all huddled together, with his legs and arms tucked up in front of him. He was naked and as wet as an eel.

They eyed each other across the room. He still hadn't spoken. She had poked him with her foot until he came round and looked up at her; then helped him up off the sand and guided him back to the cabin. The sand-grains fell off his skin as it dried out; there was no hair on his body. He sat in her chair by the window, draped in a blanket, shivering. She could see his bone-white teeth shining in his mouth. The air smelt of onions.

'Phoebe', she said, pointing at herself. Then she pointed at him, but he said nothing. 'Electra', she said, holding up the baby. He nodded and parted his lips in a slow smile; then he nodded again. She stood and put some more driftwood into the stove.

'Nearly ready', she said, pointing at the pot of soup on the hob.

Electra started to whimper. Phoebe sat back into the rocking-chair beside her bed, pulled a shawl over herself, and fed the baby. The little one stayed a long time at the breast, nodding off, then waking again to feed some more. Phoebe rocked and watched the man. He rose from the chair and fixed the blanket around his waist, tucking the edges in to hold it in place. He held up his hands to show her he meant no harm; his palms were pale. He went to the stove and ladled the soup into bowls that Phoebe had left there to warm. He knelt beside her chair and, after blowing gently on each spoonful, fed the soup into her mouth. When she was finished he ate his own. Then he pointed at himself and said 'Tam'.

It was getting dark and the water was choppy. Electra plunged out of the sea, water streeling from her long hair. Tam was scouring the sand, kicking at piles of razor shells and putting driftwood into the basket. She sneaked up behind him and launched herself at him, soaking his clothes. He roared at her, then lifted her high and marched across the sallow sand to the water. She screeched and laughed, but Tam dropped her into the waves. Electra managed to snag his leg and drag him down with her. They tumbled in the water like seal pups.

Phoebe could hear them from where she lay; every sound travelled to her. Tam had left the door open a little to let in the breeze; it carried with it the tang of seaweed, salt and oil. Her head felt hot against the pillow and her hair, which was fish-belly grey, clung to her neck. A dull light fell across the bed from the window. The cabin walls were lined with shelves, each one filled with a clutter of beach-finds: fossils, sea-urchins, lobster armour, a Jesus statue, a baby's shoe. Phoebe could see it all from her bed; each shelf a shrine of hers, or of Tam's, or of Electra's – each item weighted with memories. She could remember the day, the weather, the exact spot on the beach where everything was found; even those things that were not hers. She heard Tam whoop and, seconds later, Electra's answering laugh.

'Be careful with her, Tam', she called out, knowing he wouldn't hear; they were too far down the beach. She pushed herself up onto her elbows, reached out for her shawl. It lay over the arm of the chair and she couldn't get her fingers to grasp it. She collapsed back against the pillow, her forehead heavy with sweat. It couldn't be long now. The wind had started to lift; it was chilly. She tried again for the shawl.

Electra and Tam fell through the doorway, dripping water from their clothes and hair, giggling. Electra saw her mother's stretching hand.

'Lie back, Mama, I'll get it for you'. She plucked the shawl from the rocking-chair and tucked it around Phoebe. She pushed her soaking hair out of her eyes. 'Tam, close the door'.

He did as he was asked and then lit each of the tallow candles that stood around the room. Phoebe's chest rose and fell under the strain of her breathing.

'Get changed, both of you; this is no weather for swimming. Tam, you need to take better care of her'. She wheezed and lay back on the pillow. Her breath came in short blasts as she watched the two of them dry themselves down with towels. Tam sang as he changed out of his wet clothes; it was a song with strange words that he had told them was all about a kingdom under the sea. Phoebe felt herself getting warmer, her breath became more relaxed. She looked over at her daughter. Electra's time was coming near: the orb of her belly was stretched tight and moving lower each week; her nipples were wine-dark now, ready for the baby.

'We need to tell the midwife', Phoebe whispered, moving to make herself more comfortable under the bed-clothes.

'I'll go and tell her tomorrow', Tam said, sitting into the rocking-chair and rubbing Phoebe's hands to heat them up. She patted his arm and smiled up at him.

'Good', she said, closing her eyes, 'very good'.

Down by the shore the wind whipped at the surface of the water, tossing the waves this way and that. It reared up, howling and spinning around the cabin windows. Tam stood and lifted the broom. He swept the sand they had brought in on their feet into a pile, before hooshing it out through the door. Phoebe drifted towards sleep, and Electra sat in the chair by the window, her hands folded across the mound of her belly. She looked down towards the dark boiling sea and waited.

THE WIND ACROSS THE GRASS

You wish that someone would come in and notice the slew of spit that's rilling down your chin. You're slumped in the wheelchair, like a sack of spuds, feeling a runnel of drool slipping from your lips. You can't even lift your hand to swipe at it and the skin is getting raw. At some point they will arrive and smack a tissue across your face, tearing at the skin, and give out to you loudly.

'Look at you, Michael', they'll bawl, 'dribbling all over your nice clean shirt!'

They remind you of your mother when she'd spit on her hanky and drag it around your mouth. She'd be gripping your cheeks so hard between her fingers that your lips would stick out in a fishy pucker. But at least your mother had time for you, at least she didn't shout at you. These ones hate you; they complain to each other about how difficult you've become; about your wiry hair and your scabby arse; about your smell. You complain to yourself about their fag breath, their rough hands and their spite. You can't stand their chilly eyes.

Mostly you just sit collapsed in the chair, a lumpy collection of bones and skin, and lie to yourself about it all. There's nothing else to do. But today is Sunday. Your son will come and visit you this afternoon. He'll sit beside you and look out the window. Apart from a watery kiss when he arrives, he won't touch you. He'll talk about his work and his wife and his children and he'll glance at you to see if you react. He wants you to speak or to move, to make his visit worthwhile. He stopped bringing his family a long time ago and he doesn't even bother to make excuses for them anymore.

Part of you always wants to reach over and touch his cheek to see if it's still firm and soft like it was when he was a boy. But you know that even if you could move, you probably wouldn't. You love him, but you've never really liked him that much. Anyway, he sided with the rest of them over the house and they stole the whole lot, just like you said they would. They took it all and dumped you here.

Before you left, you walked around the room you used to share with your wife, touching the things that she had owned and loved. Framed photographs of the three of you; the ugly wooden jewellery box that she was so fond of; her hairbrush still gripping onto white hairs; her man-sized watch, the strap musky with her perfume. Your son waited for you while you wandered the house, storing up images. Now, when you think of her at all, it's not her things you remember or even the solid heft of her in your arms, but the torn face she always wore towards the end. You'd never seen this look on her before and now you can't seem to prise it from your mind. You have to strain to remember all that she used to be.

One of them comes into the room. He fiddles with the window, saying it's awful stuffy in here. You notice a long dun stain sliding down the leg of his cotton trousers; a soiling from one of the other residents, you think, or maybe just gravy slopped from his own dinner plate. Your skin feels ragged. He hasn't looked at you to notice the globs of spit gathering beneath your craw. He stamps around the room, pulling at the bedspread and emptying out the bin. When he leaves, a draught slinks across your face. You soon start to feel cold and you hope that your son will close the window when he comes.

She used to love to watch the wind across the grass. She loved nature, natural things. She would leave spaces in every day to walk the land and to stand in the fields just looking around. You often found her straddled on a fence, gazing off with a small smile patched onto her face. She made pets of all the animals and you were always telling her to stop mollycoddling them. She would only laugh. Everyone always said that she had great get-up-and-go. You were happy to stay easy and quiet but she'd drag you along with her and most of the time you were glad to follow. But you were careful in your ways and you realised after that you never gave her enough. Not ever. You never said to her to take a little extra, just for herself, and she never once asked. That pulls at you now.

Your wife is sitting across the table from you. She has a light blue apron on over her dress and her hair is pinned back at the sides. You have spent the last few hours talking about all the people you know who don't take a drink. The list is long and your wife's eyes are wet with laughter tears. Her white hands grip yours across the table and she squeezes your fingers when she laughs. You have come to the conclusion that neither of you is very fond of any of the people you have talked about. She springs from her chair and goes to the press for two glasses. She pulls a tall liqueur bottle from the top of the dresser and pours. The liquid is olivy-yellow and it gloops from the long neck of the bottle and settles into the glasses. Her mouth folds and her eyes close as she sips.

'Ugh!' she spits, and you grin at her before throwing your own measure back into your throat with a yelp.

You laugh together long and hard and you pour two more shots, knowing at least you've broken the pledge together and surely there's less harm in that?

You wonder why only the bad stuff from your young life is wedged into your head. You remember your uncle cornering you in the barn and plunging and pulling at himself while he held onto your shoulder and shouted to Jesus. The way he moved reminded you of your mother cleaving and caressing the cows' mottled teats. The same damp, shitty smells that went with the milking clutched at your nose while your uncle backed away from you, covering himself up. He told you that you were a good lad.

You can drag up the time you pushed another boy out of a tree and how he broke his arm when he hit the ground. The look on his face as he lay in the muck, with strings of snot silvering his lips, stays with you. He told on you. He said you'd pucked at him until he toppled from the branch and you swore that you hadn't.

You remember breaking all the eggs, still warm from the hens' bellies, against the back wall of the house and not being able to say why you'd done it, because you didn't know yourself. Your mother left the shell-speckled, eggy remains on the wall for days to remind you of your sin and you were given the job of scrubbing it away when the smell got high.

But somehow you can't put a proper shape on the day you married or the time when your son was born. Hardly anything is left of all the Christmases and holidays and get-togethers you had seen and you wonder why that is.

Your son is nervy when he arrives.

'Are you well, father?' he asks, and then he winces. His face is beefy. The cut of him, you think to yourself, the crude look of him. He takes his usual seat and then hops up and pushes the window wide. 'Is that alright?' he asks, and sits again, saying nothing for a while. 'Look, father', he sighs, eventually, 'I have some news'.

The words topple out of him, as heavy as rocks. He's going to London to work. They're all going, it will be a permanent move. It'll be a step-up for him and the wife. A great opportunity, he calls it, a once in a lifetime chance. But he'll try to come over once a month to see you. He knows it won't be the same as before, but he hopes that you'll understand. He doesn't want to let this one go, it's too big.

He drags his chair around so that he's facing you. He bends forward to look up into your face, his hands braced against his thighs. Your only son. His ropy hair as silver as the belly of a mackerel. Your eyes look into his, but you know that he can't read you anymore. He reaches over with his hand and passes his soft fingers across your wet chin. He pulls a hanky from his pocket and dabs at the corners of your mouth, catching the spit before it falls. He moves the hanky under your jaw and strokes at the driblets that have gathered there. Then he starts to shake and his face cracks.

'This is a shambles', he says, and he gets up and walks out of the room.

You remember something good. You remember the January morning you woke to find your room filled with a pure light. You jumped from under the eiderdown to the windowsill and looked out to see snow covering the yard. After your morning's work, your father let you and your brothers run through the fields, whooping and falling onto the cushioned ground.

The low fields had been flooded for weeks and now they were frozen over, the bullrushes stalking through the ice like soldiers. You stamped through the snow and stopped at the edge of the sheet of ice, your ears burning cold and your socks sopping inside your boots. You went first. With a mighty yowl you ran onto the ice and skidded in a long, slow glide into the middle. Your brothers laughed and shouted when they saw you and slid out after you.

Each one of you got lost in his own game after that, concentrating hard on striding and whooshing across the frozen water; lashing at the air with your arms. The clouds were combed in drifts across the sky and the sun hung red and low for hours. You glided around, your arms stretched like wings and the ice sludging in tracks behind you as the day grew shorter. You all tramped home when a fog swallowed up the river and your clothes were wringing wet. It was the best day you were ever to spend among your brothers.

You are looking forward to the end. There is too much change; too many things disturb you now and you feel that there is no place for you here. You know that you just don't fit well in the world anymore. Soon you will take your last look around; it will probably take a few months. Your son will make the trip back from London alone, no need to drag the wife and children all the way back for nothing; the nothing that all your years have made of you.

One of them comes in and snaps the window shut.

'You're perished', she says, rubbing your hands.

Then she swings out through the door leaving it hanging wide and you hear the low thrum of a television down the hall. Doors open and close, somebody laughs. It's evening and your room is dimmed by the dusk. You sit in the wheelchair, bogged down in the leatherette sling of the seat, and wait for someone to come and heave you into bed.

I, Paula

Otto thinks that I do not realise that my end is near. But, lying here now, a tired collection of skin and bones, I know I am withering away to nothing. In my mind, I see myself as I was in the summer, slipping into the Hamme, first ankle deep and then waist high. I push away from the riverbank with my toes and float on my back, letting my unpinned hair sail out from my head like a rust-coloured shawl. The egg of my belly sits high over the water and I cradle it with both hands.

Otto stands on the bank, with the Devil's Moor stretching out behind him. He flashes the brush across the canvas that squats on his easel, making lightening sketches of the boats with their black-tarred sails. I feel the river-wrack fondling my arms and the pull of the current as my hair gets heavier. Otto drags one hand across his beard and studies the canvas; he waves and calls out to me – 'Paula!' In my imaginings, I can see Elsbeth playing, the hem of her dress clotted with muck. She dips, her small face serious as she arranges her dolls in school-house rows. It's the last long hot day we are to spend together by the Hamme.

Mathilde is at my breast, crooked into my arm; she's not feeding, she lies with one tiny fist bunched beside her cheek. I am so proud of her. Of course I love Elsbeth too, with my full heart. But it's different to hold a child who is a part of your own body, who for almost a year was carried safe inside the tight drum of your belly. Elsbeth is asleep in her room off the hall, surrounded by her beloved dolls; she has welcomed Mathilde, her new half-sister, into her life, just as earlier she welcomed me as her mother.

While I lie here on this winter morning, the village of Worpswede stirs much the same as it does every day. In the poorhouse, Old von Bredow rises to tend the cow, thinking as he does about the time he spent on the shivering waves of the world's oceans. Anna Dreebeen, the dwarf, probably mutters in the half-light, pulling her blanket tight to her chest, as she waits, like me, for her days to end. All around the village her portrait decorates the walls of studios, her wide face sometimes serious, sometimes beaming. She has always been a willing model.

I know that out on the Devil's Moor the sky is heavy and ashen, but light is slowly diluting the grey. Here in our house on Hembergstrasse, Otto is stoking the fire in our room; I am pretending to sleep. I have asked Otto to hang my latest paintings on the walls, so that I might judge them while I rest. He leaves the fireplace and stands over Mathilde and me. It is a stone-cold November morning and I feel more tired than I ever have, but my mind is crowded with pictures and memories, so I let them wash over me in my half-sleep.

I wear an olive velvet dress, with a lace collar, to the gathering in Otto Modersohn's *atelier*. I arrive early and stand with my back to the wall, smoothing the nap of my skirt with my hands. My hair is slung in a low coil on my neck. The soft glow from paper lanterns makes the room shine like polished copper. Each wall is hung with Modersohn's paintings: canals, cloudscapes and orange-hued birches. Canvases recline in lazy groups against the walls. My eyes scan them; he uses oil generously, with fat brush-strokes. Modersohn paints water very well: even in summery pictures it looks icy and alive.

A table is laid with bread, meat and fruit, and there are tumblers for wine and punch. I stand, afraid to move or speak. Otto Modersohn approaches me and welcomes me to his studio with a handshake, his other hand is lost in the red folds of his beard. The warmth in his eyes touches me and I feel at ease.

'Thank you for asking me here tonight, Herr Modersohn'.

'It is my pleasure, Fraülein Becker. And I would like if you would call me Otto'.

'I hope your wife is well?'

'Helene is tired this evening, thank you for asking. She is sorry to miss the party'. He sighs. 'Come, meet my friend, Carl Vinnen'. He guides me to where Herr Vinnen sits; Vinnen stands, bows and takes my hand.

'Ah, Fraülein Becker. Modersohn tells me you are a force to be reckoned with'.

'I have my own way', I murmur.

'Well, perhaps you will let me see your work?' Vinnen says.

'I should be delighted'.

My friend, Clara, swirls through the door and joins me. She says hello and then steers me away.

'I see you have met the mighty Herr Vinnen'.

'He's asked to see my paintings'.

'Good for you', she says, finding seats for us.

We enjoy hunks of bread and spiced sausage. Vinnen has brought some bottles of French wine and he insists that we enjoy the benefit of its quality. Clara pours glass after glass until I beg her to stop. Otto Modersohn produces a guitar and sings hymns, Negro spirituals and anything else he can remember the words to. We all join in where we can, but most songs end with few singers and much laughter. Clara calls for dancing and we form circles. She invents some dances, which most people follow quite well. I find myself being partnered by Otto Modersohn; I like his quiet energy.

'Are you enjoying yourself?' he asks, above the thumping of feet as he swings me round, his hand firm on my back.

'Very much. It reminds me of parties in Bremen when I was younger. I always longed to be an adult, to take part in the real fun'.

'You come from Bremen?' asks Otto.

'I grew up there'.

'And how do you find our silent Devil's Moor after the bustle of Bremen?'

'I have found great peace here. And hope'.

Otto smiles – probably at the earnestness of my answer – and swings me faster than the beat requires, until we both laugh and have to stop dancing from dizziness. I thank him for being such an able partner and leave his side.

Otto comes to visit me; he has promised to look at my work since Herr Vinnen has told him about it. He sits in one of my little red chairs and puffs at his pipe. We drink coffee and talk; I ask after his wife. He says she is strong from the late-summer heat, but she dreads the winter. I show him my pictures one by one; he nods and has so many good comments that I have to re-look at each picture.

'You are an individual, Fräulein Becker', he says, looking at my portrait of the little knock-kneed blonde from the poorhouse. 'You're not afraid of colour'.

Of all of the artists here in Worpswede it is Otto's opinion that I value the most. I like his raw, honest representation; his landscapes are bucolic without being sentimental. I thank him for his kind words.

'It's not a case for thanks', he says, 'you have an unusual talent'.

When he leaves, I smile like a lunatic and I have to remind myself not to get a swelled head.

My companions on the train to Paris, as the new century breaks, are a travelling theatre company. They are returning to France after a Christmas tour in Germany and they bawl their way through the journey.

'Sing to us, Claudine!' shouts a black man who wears a red jacket that is bunched in creases over his big arms.

Claudine fills the carriage with bawdy songs that are squeaked through her nose and accompanied by swooping movements of her arms. Her lips are bright with carmine and bloodshot rivers decorate her eyes. The others shout the words above the singer, laughing when they come to their favourite lines.

The train lumbers on through Germany and across into Belgium, rattling by a landscape of small red houses. I sit with my hands folded in my lap, watching the performance in the carriage and growing very tired of it. Claudine changes outfit at least three times during the journey, each one more ludicrous than the last – she decorates everything with gaudy feathers – and she primps and preens herself for the delight of the black man.

He stands in the doorway, never venturing in to sit down, probably scared of my stern face.

It's dark when my creaky horse-drawn carriage finally pulls up outside the Grand Hôtel de la Haute Loire on the Boulevard Raspail; I think I will be trapped in it forever, the coachman driving me on into some endless misty night. The pink-cheeked concierge, who wears a man's overcoat over her enormous belly, leads me up five flights of steps, through a narrow stairwell, to a small room.

'You will be warm and comfortable here'.

The fireplace is empty and cold. I take my nightclothes from the trunk and dress for bed by the light of a greasy candle. Then I throw the red blanket that Otto gave me as a going-away present across the flowery coverlet. I lie, pushing back the gulps that rise in my chest, and try not to let tears break from under my lids. I close my eyes and push this place I'm in deep down inside myself, but the pillow is hard and unfamiliar and the bed too narrow. The tension of the journey will not leave my body, so I sit up and write a short note to my family to let them know that I have arrived safely. My throat feels ragged when I lie down again.

I pause to breathe deeply. Laying my hand on the railing that runs alongside the steps, I turn to look at the city scattered below like a toy town; each dome, spire and cluster of buildings looks as small as a matchbox. On I go up the steep steps until I come to a sloping street that has small houses tumbling down both sides; the sails of a windmill chop the air above my head. I am on a small square where chickens rush and peck in the dirt. My breathing catches and I stop; the birds lash their beaks at my shoes and then scuttle away when I shake my toes at them. They burble and cluck with annoyance, scrabbling alongside each other.

The pale domes of the Sacré Coeur, the still unfinished basilica, stand guard above the laneways of Montmartre; I am awed by its size and solemnity. I've heard that it's possible to eat cheaply in the refectory. I creep into the church, unused to the smell of the incense that smokes from a censer by the altar. Candlelight dances across golden mosaics and there is a deep silence among those solitary people who are huddled in prayer. I look up at grim statues of Jesus: his torn face and bleeding side. An old nun steps from a confessional and smiles at me.

'Welcome', she says, her voice filling the church to the roof. I nod at her and smile. 'You are not French', she says, taking my hands in her own fleshy ones. Nodding again, I whisper that I am German. 'Our near neighbours', she says. 'Come and have something to eat. My name is Sister Valentine'.

I follow her into the refectory where there is a clutter of long tables and benches. Only one person sits there: an old man with a face like an onion. He lifts his head from the soup he's slurping and smiles at me. Sister Valentine puts me sitting down and returns with a steaming bowl of soup and two hunks of bread. I think she means to watch me eat, but instead she sits with the old man and they begin to pray in that animated Catholic way: eyes closed, shoulders swinging, their words rising and falling together. Their chant is soothing.

I eat the soup greedily, glad that there is no one to watch my hunger. My whole body has become skinny and ugly lately, and the hot meat soup is just what I need to feel stronger. I eat more slowly and mop up the rest of the soup with a fat piece of bread.

'Have you had enough to eat, Fraülein?' the old nun asks.

'Yes, thank you very much'.

I smile at her use of German, grateful that she wants to make me feel welcome. I just hope she doesn't try to convert me, like the ugly monk who hops around Notre Dame preaching madly against us Protestants.

'I hope we will see you here again'.

I slip back through the hush of the church and into the cool evening air. I bounce down the steps away from the Sacré Coeur through a tangle of streets to rue Lafitte, hoping that Ambroise Vollard's little gallery will still be open; it is.

'You have returned, Mademoiselle', Monsieur Vollard says, looking up from his desk; his voice crinkles like brown paper.

He knows I will not buy – he's used to browsers – and he waves his hand to indicate that I'm welcome to look around. I go straight to the back of the shop to find the canvases I saw the last time; they are still stacked, face to the wall, and I enjoy turning them around and lining them up. They are extraordinary, overflowing with the modernity my father warns me away from. I particularly like a landscape with trees that has a village lying low in the background. The foreground – as well as the roofs of the houses – glows with burning shades of ochre and sienna and the leaves on the trees are a blur of muted greys and greens. This is what I too want to achieve, *must* achieve, with my own painting.

'Cézanne', says a voice behind me. I turn to see Vollard standing nearby watching me. 'Paul Cézanne is the artist's name'.

'French?'

'*Mais oui*'.

Vollard smiles and slinks back to his desk. I turn around some more of this Cézanne's pictures – it's easy to tell which are his – and step back to study them. His still-life studies are not still at all – they pulse with life – and his use of colour is bold and moody. He is able to reduce each object in a painting to a simple shape, but somehow everything is held together perfectly. Each apple in a painting of his is an apple in its own right, but it sits easily with every other bright apple on a plate.

Carefully replacing the canvases, I thank Monsieur Vollard and leave. A quiet happiness burbles through me; I have found something that will help with my own work, and now I know that the things *I* feel I want to show in my own paintings are possible. I skip back over the Seine to my little room, stopping under the archway by the concierge's door to play for a while with her haughty grey cat.

Lying back on my red blanket and fingering its woolliness, I decide I will reply to the birthday letter I received from Otto Modersohn. It is such a lovely letter, open and warm; he sends wishes 'from his heart' for my body and soul and for my artistic life. He says that it would be lovely if I was to return to Worpswede soon, but also that he would like to be in Paris to share my enjoyment of it. He hints that he might come, with some of the others, to see the World Exposition.

I talk to him in my letter about art; it is easier to relate these things to him, rather than to my family, because I know he understands. I tell him about my trips to the Louvre, about how moved I am by the Venus de Milo, how I love the way she holds her head as if she is listening intently to someone, a person she knows well; I write that I like the way the drapes at her hips look as if they will slip at any second. I describe the delicate red-haired girls in one of Botticelli's Florentine frescoes and say that Otto's little daughter Elsbeth – whose hair is a similar colour – will probably grow up to be as beautiful. I bend forward to sniff at the posy of violets I have in a glass on the windowsill and continue writing.

'I am surrounded by flowers here; they are so very inexpensive and I always must buy some to brighten my room when I pass the flower-sellers on the bridges over the river. They are the one natural thing that Parisians cling to among all this stone and filth and movement. The French are so blasé and full of gaiety, they make me feel quite stolid and ponderous. We Germans could learn a lot from them, especially from that certain lightness in their art'.

I ask after the health of Helene and promise to send her a bunch of pink Paris roses; they are so pretty here: tightly budded and slow-blooming. I tell him a little about my classes at the Colarossi; I say that I would very much like to know what he is painting now. I promise Otto that I will return to Worpswede – saying how much I love it there – once I have progressed a little more in Paris.

Then I tell him what I have told nobody else so far, not even my family; the small piece of news I have been holding close to myself and smiling about: at the *concours* in the Académie, I won the medal. Each of the four teachers voted for me. I am proud about it, of course, but also a little shy. I can't help wondering, somewhere in the recesses of my mind, if I deserve it, if I have achieved enough to merit it. But, on the other hand, I feel that winning the medal helps me to know that I will be able to climb the mountain and see from the top what it is I will go on to achieve. Really the medal has nothing to do with what I have learnt or what I will learn, but I feel I am getting somewhere and it gives me the strength to keep going. There will be plenty of mountains to climb, but I will take each one as I come to it.

My soul is soaring: my Worpswede friends are coming to Paris. I have written to each of them about the World Exposition and now they say they must take the trip to see it themselves. Otto Modersohn will come, though at first he said he preferred to remain a hermit in Worpswede, probably out of consideration for his Helene, who has been very ill again.

On their first night, I take the Worpsweders to the Bullier dancehall. It is a picturesque sprawl of a place, tucked behind the Boulevard Raspail, packed each evening with laughing laundry girls and lean artists, dancing, drinking and sitting head-to-head. We find a table near the back of the hall and Otto orders wine for us. Frau Bock and I watch a student – in a plum-coloured velvet suit and slouchy hat – swirl a merry blonde, who is wearing silly cycling bloomers, around the floor; their smiles are wide and their movements vast. The man stops and bows to the girl and she throws her body forward in an elaborate curtsey; then they fall into each other's arms and giggle. Otto laughs. We raise our glasses and drink to Germany.

'To the Fatherland!' Herr Bock says.

'To the Motherland!' I correct him, and we all clink glasses and swallow hard.

'To art, and all who are in her thrall', Otto says, and tips his glass to mine.

'Yes, to art', I whisper, glancing first at Otto, then at Frau Bock, who is beaming at me across the rim of her glass. She sends a slow wink and I smile, then ask her what she thought of the Exposition.

When the others are not around, Otto and I belong together. We do not say anything about it, but our silent agreement states to me that we want nothing more than to be close to each other. His room is in my *hôtel*, and so we start and end each day nearby. My breath catches in my neck every morning when I wake and slowly remember that he is in the same building, sharing the same air as me. Often we have coffee and rolls together before meeting the others.

He has stood in the doorway of my room in the evening, to admire my posies or to see what I have been working on. His physical presence thrills some deep, hidden part of me: that piece of me that spreads from my mind, through my bones, right down my stomach, to my pelvis. When he is near, every bit of my body seems to flush and fill with blood; all I want is to listen to his voice and observe the curl of his hair on his collar, or see the scatter of freckles that decorates the back of his hands.

We return to the Haute Loire arm-in-arm; I am laughing at Otto, he is doing an impression of Herr Bock, gurning his lips and crinkling his eyes in that overly serious way that Bock has. I beg him to stop because my chest is sore from laughing; he does it again and giggles convulse me as we arrive at the *hôtel*. The concierge meets us; her eyes are thrown down and she holds an envelope.

'Herr Modersohn …' she says, hands it to him and steps back.

It's a telegram. Otto thanks her, puts it into his pocket and gestures for me to mount the stairs before him. I walk ahead, my guts burning, and stop outside my own room.

'Come with me, Paula, while I open it', he says.

I follow him into his room; it's cool in there – he has left the window ajar – and there is a faint smell of oranges. I stand by the door, turning my fingers around and around each other. His back is to me and the paper rustles when he opens the envelope. I see him read it, but he says nothing, doesn't move.

'Otto?'

'Helene is dead'.

He turns to me, his face torn; I run to him and take his crumpling body in my arms. Our knees give way and we sink on to the edge of the bed; Otto's head lands in my lap and he sobs and shudders, his tears darkening my skirt. I stroke his hair, tamp it down with my hand, and hush him.

My room in Worpswede is quiet. I can hear the walls breathing and, off in the distance, the burr and hum of the village: children laughing, the rumble of cart-wheels, birdsong. I am afloat in my bed, the fever making the room pitch and swell for a while, like a boat. I feel the bed take to the air and hover, before slumping back to the floor. Then all is easy again and my mind becomes sensible. I would like some bread dipped in milk, but when I try to rise, my limbs feel as soft as flower stems, and I fall back against the sheets. My eyes try to focus on my easel, the rush-seated chair, the milky-glassed mirror and some new paintings I have hung. Then it all starts to bend and sway; I have to close my eyes to feel normal. Cold tears slide into my ears.

Because the doctor has ordered bed-rest, my father has said I may be calm and restful for a while, and must not worry for the moment about returning to Bremen to find work. I think about this as I jolt in and out of sleep and wonder if I should enjoy being a governess to a family of small children. I dream that I am surrounded by little ones: they pull at my skirts, whinging and whining, and over their tawny heads I can see my easel, idle in the corner. I wake sweating. I'm not sure if a day, an hour or a week has gone by, but Otto is standing in the middle of the room, looking at me. I try to sit up.

'Otto, I …'

'Lie back, Paula'. He puts his big hand under the back of my head and eases me down onto the pillow. 'I'm here, I'm here, relax, lie back. There now'.

Otto pulls the chair over to my bedside and holds my hand. I push out a laugh – to show my embarrassment at my dishevelled room and self – but it emerges as a strangled-up croak; he pats my arm and tells me not to speak.

He comes every day after that, sitting by me long into the evening, my door open to the July heat. He reads to me from Knut Hamsun's *Pan* and I lie back and listen, feeling a little strength returning to my veins and bones, day by day.

'I know that I won't live very long', I say to him one evening, when I feel tired again after days of feeling well. Otto lays down the book; I am lying on my bed, outside the covers, clothes and boots on.

'Really, Paula, such a thing to say'. He looks flustered and I feel foolish, thinking of Helene, but then I can't seem to stop myself from going on.

'Oh, I know it sounds silly, but I feel my life will be a short, intense celebration, rather than a languid, long-lived affair'. I look up into his face. 'It's just what I feel'.

Otto smiles, a small sad smile. 'Well, I hope you live to be one hundred and thirty-five and that I am there beside you, cheering you on'.

I take his hand and lift it to my cheek. He strokes my skin with the rough pads of his fingers. I look at his face, the kind eyes, and think *I have fallen in love with you, Otto Modersohn.*

'Read on, dear friend', I say and, lifting the book, Otto pushes his spectacles onto the bridge of his nose.

'I would like to paint you, Paula', he says, before beginning to read, and I blush and squeeze his arm.

We walk through blue moonlight, the trees stretching above us and making dapples on our faces each time we reach a clearing. Otto waits for me when I fall behind; I am still not fully strong. Then he takes my arm and guides me along the forest path. The night smells clay-rich, earthy, and it is nicely humid. We talk about this and that while we walk, telling stories from our past lives. I tell him about the death of my cousin Cora, whom I loved, in the sandpit where we played.

'It was a beautiful place: a natural sandpit sheltered among trees. We went there a lot – the sand twirled in luminous heaps and we buried ourselves in it, playing pirates and slaves. There were seven of us there that day; we were merry and laughing. We had covered ourselves in the sand, up to our necks, all around the sides of the pit. Cora was further down, below us. The sand shifted and she just seemed to be sucked into the centre of the pit: a vortex opened up, like a whirlpool in the sea, and she was gone. I hid my face – I knew something terrible had happened, but I didn't know what to do. So I hid my eyes. All the others were screaming, but I covered my face'. I look at Otto; his dear face is worried. 'It was the first real tragedy in my life and I think of it often'.

Otto stops, lays down his bundle, and puts his arms around my waist; it reminds me of when we danced together at the gathering in his *atelier* and I felt his hands burn through my dress to the skin of my back. I slip my arms up around his neck and put my head to his chest.

'There will be no more tragedies, I hope', he whispers into my hair, and I hug him close, feeling his long body tight to mine. We walk on and stop at a deep part of the birch forest where a natural hollow has formed. The moon is directly above, dropping its light down on us.

'Is this the place?' I ask, and Otto nods.

He lays a blanket out in the upper dip of the hollow and I begin to undress. Otto kicks the legs of his easel to make it stand and pulls the brushes and paints from his canvas roll. I shiver, though it's a warm night, and feel the pucker of my hardening nipples. When my clothes are in a squat pile, I stand with my hands covering my belly and wait. Otto motions to me to sit; he arranges me on the blanket and I hear him gasp quietly when his fingers touch the soft flesh of my upper arm. He asks me to lie down in the end, has me recline like Venus or Olympia, and places one hand behind my head.

'Unpin your hair', he says. I do as he asks and my hair topples over my shoulders and down my back. He lifts handfuls of it and arranges it so that one breast is covered, the other bare. 'There now', he says, and returns to his easel.

BABY PEACOCKE

My name's Baby Peacocke and I live with my Ma. I'm fifty-odd. We've been in our van for yonks and we share the bedroom. You're thinking, 'She's gonna spill her stupid guts now', but I'm not. And I might. I was only going to talk about my Ma for a bit, and the way she's lived into her nineties; of all the people I know my Ma's the one who got given that grace. I was going to tell you about Brian too.

Years pass real quick and you'd think that a person would get to their ninety-fourth year in a bang and a flash. But, no, it's a long time to live, if you really sit and think about it. For myself, I don't see why someone like my Ma lives so long, when perfectly decent people drop dead, or are murdered, every day. It's one of those mysteries that I'm always trying to answer. It does me no good. It's not that she's bad – not at all – she just wears me out. This is my Ma's favourite conversation:

'I suppose any day now some fella will come and sweep you away. Ah well, what harm?'

'Hardly, Ma'.

'You'll up and leave me, as sure as shit stinks'.

'No, Ma, I won't'.

'I hope he has all his own teeth, for your sake'.

'Oh, here we go. And who exactly *is* this famous fella with the teeth, Ma?'

'Ah now, Baby, you know better than anyone'.

'I don't'.

Then she starts talking like there's someone else in the van with us: 'I can barely move my poor bones and she's going to leave me here to rot. Upping and leaving me she is'.

'I'm stopping here with you, Ma', I say, not missing my cue. It's like we've been rehearsing a play for thirty years.

We have the only caravan in town, since the Travellers' parking spot was blocked off with boulders. Our van squats on the edge of the site where my Da half-built a bungalow before my Ma threw him out; after a beating that left her with a fractured skull. He went to England.

The bungalow's empty windows gape at the traffic on the dual carriageway and the bare rafters are as pale as moth wings from the rubbing weather. Our van looks like a huge beetle hunched in the dry grass by the roadside, at the far end of the site from the house. But it's neat; I keep the windows bright, and I've flanked the steps to the door with buckets of flowers and shrubs.

There's a cross near our van; a mock-Celtic cross, badly carved from a single sheet of wood. The varnish on it is brittle and peeling; the whole thing is crusted with muck and there are rotting, yellow-cellophaned flowers tied to it with ribbon.

'He'll be here today with fresh flowers', I say to my Ma.

'He will. Ask him in'.

The father of the boy comes up on the bus once a month to change the flowers. And say a prayer for his son. He's a widower, as young as myself.

'It's desperate, isn't it?'

Ma nods. 'Ask him in'.

The man steps up into the stale heat of the van and pulls the door shut.

'This is cosy', he says, looking at the tiny kitchen and the ordered clutter on the shelves in the living-room – China couples, hardbacks, framed photographs. He holds out his hand. 'I'm Brian Coogan'.

My Ma sits on a narrow wedge of banquette, looking up at him. Her long hair is clipped back on each side of her forehead and it's dark with grease. She looks elegant in that half-mad way she has.

'Eleanor Peacocke. And this is Baby'.

He nods. 'It's great in here, Mrs Peacocke – everything's only a reach away', he says.

'I love my old van. You wouldn't get me into a house again for all the turf in Ireland. Call me Eleanor; I wasn't christened Mrs Peacocke'.

'We're sorry about your boy, Mr Coogan', I say, handing him a cup of tea.

He nods and takes the tea. 'It's Brian, please'.

'I believe every road in the country is decorated with crosses and shrines, Brian', my Ma says, 'we're living in one massive graveyard'. She holds her palsied left arm up with her right hand, to give it an appearance of life.

'It can seem like that', Brian says, and he smiles at me.

He leaves, promising to drop in when he comes up from Offaly next month, to visit his son's cross.

I unwind the helix of my Ma's plait, separating each section of hair into a bumpy tail. I take the comb and run it over it; it slides through the grease.

'Is he the kind of man you'd marry?'

'Who?'

'Who! Who! Don't act the thick with me, Baby'.

I smack her crown gently with the comb. 'I'm too old. And I've seen too many rotten marriages to be interested, Ma'.

'Don't underestimate marriage – didn't Grace Gifford marry Joseph Mary Plunkett hours before he was executed? Why would she do that?' She looks at me in the mirror, trying to get me to look at her, but I go on combing her hair. 'Because marriage is *important*, that's why. It has *meaning*'. She tilts back her head, enjoying the comb's teeth raking over her scalp. 'They weren't even allowed to speak to each other during the ceremony. Grace was brought to see Joseph later that night, for ten minutes. Imagine – only a few minutes with her husband. They murdered him an hour or so later in the stonebreakers' yard in the jail'. She waves her hand. 'Ah, you're young – you don't care about things like that'.

'Young? Come off it, Ma'.

'"*A model husband runs all his wife's errands, pays all her bills, and cries like a child at her death*". I read that somewhere. Keep it in mind now for Brian'.

'I barely know the man and you have me dead and him a widower. Thanks'. I lift her hair between my fingers and let it fall; I like its smell, it reminds me of raisins: old and sweet and heavy with dirt. 'You'll have to lean over the sink for the first rinse'.

She grunts, gets up and crouches over the tiny sink. It takes a few jugs of water to soak the length of her hair and she moans about it being too hot and too cold. She pants with the effort of her scrunched position and sits back onto the stool, wheezing. I squeeze a blob of shampoo onto her head.

'Oh! That's freezing', she says.

'Shut up, you're like a three-year-old'. I massage her scalp, fluffing the foam into peaks.

'You should wash your own hair, Baby. Never mind me; I don't need to be clean where I'm going. Get yourself looking nice for you-know-who'.

It's Brian's day to come and visit the cross; Ma says we have to dress up.

She picks up a fawn bra and throws it at me. 'Them hooks are hard to do up at the best of times, never mind if you're a cripple like me'.

Wearing a bra is her idea of being dressed-up.

'Come on so'.

'Close the curtains first', she says, and I yank them shut.

She wiggles out of the dressing gown. I come up behind her, tell her to lean forward, and then sling the bra around her body, catching a strap on either side of her.

'Now, lift yourself in', I say, 'one at a time'.

I catch the warm, sharp smell from her body: lemon layered over vinegary sweat. Ma hauls one breast up with her right hand, tucking it into the cup, then the other. She snorts. I flick her hair to one side and clip the hooks in place across her back. I lift her dead left arm into one sleeve of her blouse. It's heavy and the skin is mottled a purple-red; it feels cold like meat. Sliding her right arm into the other sleeve, she looks up into my face and watches me do up the buttons.

'He'd do as a husband. Someone to mind you after I'm gone'.

Brian asks to look at the bungalow that Daddy built; he says he might be able to fix it up. Then we could sell it and make money. The pair of us walk across the strip of land behind the van. It's dusk-dark, my favourite time of the day, full of promise; mornings are cold and empty, like buckets waiting to be filled.

'You never had any children, Baby. You didn't marry'.

I look sideways at him, at his stomach bursting against the check shirt. 'I didn't get a chance, Brian. Mammy has always needed minding'.

'Would you have liked to have kids?'

'I'm not sure that I'd have made a great mother; I might have turned into my Ma. I'd have been afraid of that'.

'You seem to me to get on. Do you not?'

'Mammy is changeable: up one minute, down the next. She's always *at* me. There were two of us – two girls – and she had time for only one: my sister Rose. Rose could do no wrong'. We stop under the orange glow of a street-lamp. 'Mammy couldn't stand my father. Me, she disliked. She used to say that I looked like Daddy with long hair'. I sigh. 'She was fond of saying, "Ugly girls need a talent", as a way of explaining why I alone was sent to piano lessons. I loved the piano but Rose tormented me over it. She was jealous'.

'What was your father like?' Brian looks at me, right into my eyes, sort of scaring me. But I look straight back, liking his pug nose and the pouchy bulge of his cheeks.

'It's hard to say what way Daddy was. He let her bully us. She wanted him to stand up to her, you know, but he never really did. He lashed out in the end – hit her – then did a runner'.

'That was hard'. Brian licks his lips, a poky little tongue-tip swipe.

'He never laid a finger on us. My sister used to beat me though, slyly. I'd be covered in bruises, but she knew I wouldn't tell'. I stop talking, feeling silly for saying so much. 'What about you? Was he your only son?' I point at the cross that comes into view every time a car's headlights pass over it. Brian shakes his head; he doesn't want to talk about it.

I step inside the shell of the bungalow and look around at the grey walls and the hole for the fireplace. I smell the night: cold clearness and earth, petrol fumes. Stands of weeds clutter the doorway and I bend to pull a few. Brian comes up behind me and puts his hands on my hips, his front to my backside. I can feel the hard length of him pressing through my skirt. I stand slowly and turn to him; his trousers are around his ankles and his shirt ends don't cover him up. He grabs my head and pulls my lips onto his; he forces his tongue between my teeth and his front against mine. He pushes his legs against mine and I can feel him: hot, alive, animal. He jiggles against me, does a short moan, then steps back.

'I'm sorry, Baby', he says, and his face is shocked. He goes to turn away.

'Brian', I say, trying to take his hand, but he bends, pulls up his trousers and walks off.

I stand in the doorway of the house, watching him slope like a shadow towards the town and the bus-stop; then I go back to the van.

'I suppose you'll put me in an old folks' home, with the money you get when you sell the bungalow', Ma says, without turning her face from the television.

'Oh, shut up, will you?' I say, going to the back of the van to change my skirt.

'I'm going to a recital in the city next weekend. Would you like to come?' Brian says.

'Me? Ah, no'. I look at the floor. 'Sure what would I wear?'

'Go on, we'll find you something to wear'. Ma rubs her bad arm. 'Will you go?'

I look at Brian. 'I will so'.

The church is half-full when we get there; Brian links me up the aisle. I pull at my ponytail, fixing it over my breast, and smooth the front of my dress. It has lines of silver puckered through it and it might be too flash; I pick at the buttons and pluck at the waist.

'Don't worry, you look smashing', Brian says.

'Stop codding me; I look like mutton'.

He guides me into the front pew. 'It's better to sit up here because of the acoustics – you can't hear a thing if you're too far back'.

The musicians are in front of the altar, lit up on all sides by glowing candles; they hold their instruments and look at the audience. The church goes dim; the only light comes from the flowing candles and the yellow strips on the music stands. The violinist sits with her legs planted wide, her feet on tip-toe. She bends to the microphone and introduces the Shostakovich piece they'll play first, explaining that it's quite a melodic piece for the composer. Making eye contact with the other musicians, she draws herself up with a deep breath and brings her bow across the strings.

I settle back. When I listen to music on the radio in the van, I like to close my eyes and let it waft through me. Now I'm fascinated to watch the musicians, throwing themselves into the piece – with all their privilege and talent – right in front of me. I can't take my eyes off the violinist, she looks like she's possessed. Her eyes roll and her body moves with the heaving emotion of the music, changing with each tempo. The violin looks like it's part of her. I wonder if I'd kept up my piano playing, whether I ever would've played like that: with my whole body a writing part of it. I doubt it; that sort of madness would've been stamped out of me one way or another, by my Ma, or by myself.

Everyone's clapping and Brian's looking at me; I realise I've slipped off the pew, and am kneeling down, with my hands clasped, as if I'm praying.

We give Brian the money to do the bungalow and he starts on it right away; the strip of land between the van and the house is a mess of cement mixer and sand and breeze-blocks. Men come and go, mixing and slooshing and banging. They carry pipes and shovels and they drink tea made on our stove, standing around outside the van, trying not to curse while they talk.

Brian comes to speak to us. The bungalow's rafters are weak.

'They're as soft as dust, Eleanor', he says to Ma, 'from the exposure'.

'I'll have the money by Friday', Ma says.

Brian collects the money and says he has a big job on in Offaly and he'll see us again in a few days. He winks at me as he steps down out of the van.

After he's gone, we sit watching headlights spin across the ceiling, listening to the thrumming cars pass.

'That's the last we'll see of him', Ma says.

'I suppose it is', I say.

FEEDER

When you think one thing is the worst thing someone has ever done to you, then they do something worse again, you have to adjust your mind to that. To the second thing. You have to wipe out the first grudge and fill in the space with this much weightier sin of theirs. That's what I had to do with what my sister Rena did to me. She still thinks it was Bob's your uncle, A-OK, but it bloody well wasn't.

'I don't see why you're getting your knickers in a knot', Rena said, 'he's never going to know. They remember nothing'.

I sat on her sofa. 'But *I* know; *I'll* remember', I said. 'Jesus, I think I'm going to puke'. I put my hand over my mouth and swung my head between my legs.

'Less of the amateur dramatics, Clodagh, if you don't mind'.

I told them at my La Leche League group. The older ones kept their faces rigid, like good Castleknock ladies. These are the ones who will never discuss anything real: with them there is no talk of sex or uncooperative bodily functions or money. Nothing that might stink. The lone parent girl, what's-her-name, had the good grace to look shocked; she hugged her baby tighter in case one of us swooped in. Our one and only working-class mammy looked as benign as the poshies and said, 'I think it's cool', which annoyed me. Célina, our League leader, said, 'Well, it was bet-ter than giving 'im a bott-ell'. She's French and a breast-feeding zealot; which I am kind of for and against. You should only take it so far.

I think about Rena's fat, impossible nipple pressed into my baby's gorgeous mouth. And that the betraying little bastard took it! Rena's milk flowing down his tender throat; her Riesling and poached salmon flavoured milk. How could he have accepted her? Her nipples are brown and long – nothing like mine – they look like a sow's dugs. I imagine Rena's nipples tasting of fags; I see them puffing like two horizontal chimneys, my baby's mouth full of nicotined smoke that turns his face blue.

Rena always acts as if she knows more than me about everything, and as if we are closer than we are. If she wasn't my sister, I'd actually *hate* her. She does the big sister thing, whereby I'm a helpless eejit who is to be laughed at. 'That's so Clodagh', she'll say, 'over re-acting, as usual. Being a drama queen'.

I have to turn my eyes away when Katie runs to Rena and pulls out her boob for a crafty, unnecessary suck; I don't know which upsets me more: my sister's creamy, veined breast, or her walking-talking daughter acting the baby.

But my baby, oh my baby – he is living perfection. If not very picky when it comes to comforters.

'He was in bits', Rena said, 'crying like a weasel'.

'You should've rang me, I'd have come back'.

'But you'd have taken at least half an hour to get here, Clodagh'.

'I don't give a fuck. You don't *do* that. You don't stick your tit in someone else's baby's mouth!'

'Phuh', she says, with an incredulous gape. She clearly thinks I'm nuts.

I pick up the baby and unhook the front of my nursing bra; he latches on instantly, his mouth like a split cherry around the areola. He snuffles and gulps *uh-uh-uh* and I gaze at him; I feel the weight of his head on my arm, his tongue pulling the milk from me. My breast is goosebumped like seersucker and the baby's fat hand rests there proprietorially. Then he stops feeding, tilts his head back and opens his mouth; the sucking blister on the purse of his lips rises in a dark peak and he smiles his milky madman's smile. I kiss his hard little forehead and he head-butts my breast, clamps on again with a deep breath, and gives me an upturned eye. I am completely and happily at his mercy. And I forgive him.

Ms De'Ath

Vanessa's hands are squat: her fingers lie like a brace of bonnavs suckling at the sow of her palm; she studies them, then licks the heel of her left hand and rubs her eye with it – the wetness lessens the dry pull of the skin.

Vanessa is sitting on the top deck of a bus that is barrelling along the quays; she listens to the Christchurch bells and remembers kissing Jared in the laneway below the cathedral, under a rainy sky. The same musical bellowing had sounded as their tongues met and they had both laughed, startled and pleased. The bus stops and, staring down onto the heads of the alighting passengers, she thinks of another morning, a few months ago, when they held one another under the Spire: lips bunched together, nose-to-cold-nose, arms tight around each other, eventually having to pull away. Always separating. He had gone home and she had eaten salty eggs, alone in a café on North Earl Street.

She feels tired: her back and eyelids ache. The bus hurtles on and Vanessa stares down into the murky river. I can't be away from Jared, she thinks, I'm like a book with no binding without him. Like a sea with no horizon; a candle without a flame. She sighs. An old man slumps into the seat beside her and she has to drag her hand-bag from under his backside.

'Do I have to pay extra to sit beside you?' he says, and cackles, showing butter-yellow teeth.

The man reeks: a mix of yesterday's whiskey, chip-shop stink and unwashed skin. Vanessa turns her head away and looks at her nails: like her fingers, they are stubby, ugly; powdered with white flecks. Maybe she should have painted them this morning, made them a bit prettier. For Jared. She thinks of his voice, the way he skates over his words, elongating the vowels, dragging out each syllable. His beautiful, sweet voice that is peppered with curses and, sometimes, words she has never heard before.

The old man leans matily into her side. 'Cheer up, love, it might never happen', he says, and starts to sing *The Galway Shawl*.

'It already has', she says, more to herself than to him.

Vanessa watches Parkgate Street flitting by, then the sturdy-walled Phoenix Park with the phallus of the Wellington monument at its edge. This is the landscape of my childhood, she thinks, and folds her hands across her stomach.

There were cobwebs hammocked from the ceiling in each of the corners of the waiting room; Vanessa stared at them – a magazine lifeless in her lap – and imagined that they were full of skin particles, human dust.

'Ms Vanessa De'Ath?' called a man's voice.

'Yes, that's me'.

Vanessa rose from the chair. The magazine slipped to the floor and she scrabbled to retrieve it. She wanted to cry. By the time she looked up, the man had disappeared behind the door; Vanessa pushed it wide and followed a dim corridor to an open doorway. She stood there, looking in.

'Sit down, please'. Vanessa entered the room and sat in front of a desk; the man sat opposite her. 'Now', he said, making a steeple of his fingers, 'first things first. That is to say, we'll get the "legal" bit out of the way before anything else'. He sniggered. 'Basically, I need you to sign this form'.

She nodded and took the pen he held out to her. Jared and Cristina's signatures were already on the page. The looping 'J' in Jared's name comforted Vanessa for a moment and she scribbled her own name as close as she could to his. The man put out his hand for the pen and pointed with it to the curtained bed in the corner.

'Do I lie down?' she asked.

He sighed elaborately and frowned at her. 'Strip off, put on the gown and hop up on the bed. The nurse will be with you in a jiff. She'll be doing the procedure', he poked the pen into his breast pocket, 'not me'.

The bus scuds along towards Chapelizod, emptying and refilling itself at each new stop. The old man's head lolls against Vanessa's shoulder and she jerks it to try to rouse him. His smell, and the way his red scalp shows through greasy hair-strands, makes a familiar queasiness rise in her throat. When his head slumps forward, skimming her breast, she pokes him hard with her fingers and he wakes up saying 'What?' He looks at her through slitted eyes for a few seconds, then pulls himself out of the seat and lurches down the stairs.

Vanessa breathes through her nose and puffs out through her lips; she cradles her swollen belly with her hands and tries to calm the nausea. By controlling her breathing in the way she has been taught, the churning in her guts backs away. She had hoped the sickness would pass after the first three months, but it was proving to be relentless. Leaning forward, over her bump, she whispers, 'There now, baby, there now'. A boy sitting across the aisle from her slides open a window and Vanessa closes her eyes, bathing in the breeze that blows through the bus.

The nurse's hands were as cold as a fish. Vanessa lay on her back, legs parted.

'Just relax', the nurse said, 'let your legs fall wider, that's it'. She held onto one of Vanessa's knees and the suck of her latexed fingers echoed around the room. 'Now we're ready', she said, and smiled. 'Have you got someone with you?' Vanessa shook her head and turned her face to the wall. 'Oh, I'm sorry, I shouldn't have asked that'.

'It's OK'.

'I am sorry though, we're not really meant to chat with the patients, and that was a silly thing to say'.

'It's fine', Vanessa managed a smile, 'I'm fine'.

When the nurse had finished, she brought a wheelchair to the bedside.

'In you get. I've to bring you to the ward for your rest'.

'I can walk'.

'You're not allowed to. Anyway, it sort of helps things along if you stay sitting or, preferably, lying down'. She patted her arm. 'But if you *are* going to sit, keep your legs up, OK?'

Vanessa allowed herself to be trundled along in the wheelchair; once she was in bed, she asked the nurse to pull the curtains around her cubicle. She dozed into a stiff sleep and, during it, felt noise and movement in the room. When she woke up, Jared was sitting by the bed.

'Hello there', he said, and kissed her cheek.

'Oh, you're here'.

'Sorry I missed the … operation. How are you feeling?'

'I'm grand', she shifted onto her side to look at him, 'it's not what you'd call major surgery. You look nice'.

'Thank you'. Jared smiled down at her and rubbed his forehead. 'No regrets?'

Vanessa squeezed his fingers. 'None'.

Jared was holding Cristina on the sofa, half-lying down, his legs tucked around her waist. She was saying again how she wanted to be a part of the pregnancy, to be a player in it; almost as if the baby were growing under her own skin. She said she would like to monitor the progress, witness the changes.

'I want to meet this Vanessa, get to know her, help her. I want to see what she's like, for God's sake'. She bent her head back to look up into his face.

'It's better that you don't meet her; it would only fuck things up. I've vetted her – she's fine, trust me'. He kissed the top of her head. 'Anyway, as she gets bigger – more obviously pregnant-looking – people we know might see you with her and put two-and-two together. We'd be found out'. Jared kissed Cristina on the neck, called her his little pet, and told her to let him handle it.

'But, what is she like? At least describe her to me'.

'You've seen her photograph, she's like a younger version of you. Stop being silly, Cristina. Jesus'.

'You can't tell anything from a photo. What kind of an accent does she have, for example? How does she act? Is she bright? Healthy?' She rubbed the length of his legs. 'Please, Jar, I need to know that she's … special. Special enough to be one half of our baby'.

Jared hugged her. 'She's special, OK? She really is. Just trust me on this'.

Vanessa got to the hotel before him; she explored the room, tested the springiness of the mattress, and touched the boxed products in the bathroom: bath-foam, shower cap, a tiny sewing kit. O'Connell Street hummed below the window, all its busy inhabitants crossing from side to side, each with their own purpose. The room was quiet, spotless, a little old-fashioned; Vanessa liked the swagged curtains and the honey-striped wallpaper. She had never stayed in a hotel in Dublin city before – it seemed a decadent thing to do, to stay in a hotel in your hometown. Jared arrived a little late, looking handsome in his business suit, she thought. He brought her a bar of dark chocolate and a bunch of purple freesias; their smell made her head swoon, but she loved them and thanked him over and over.

'How's the tummy?' he asked.

'Good today'. Vanessa sat on the side of the bed, watching him, and twirled a lock of hair through her fingers.

'I'm glad'. Jared bent over, pushed her back against the pillows and kissed her stomach. 'Hello little one'.

He lifted her T-shirt and flicked his tongue around her belly button, then undressed her bit by bit. Moving over her slowly, gently, he asked her all the time if she was OK. She nodded to let him know that she was and drank him in with her eyes. Afterwards, he held her in his arms and stroked the swell of her ripening stomach.

'I hope the baby gets your skin', he said, 'all creamy-soft and perfect'.

'And *your* smile', Vanessa said, 'you have such a lovely smile'.

'And your hands'.

'No! My hands are horrible'. She held them up. 'They're like table-tennis paddles'.

Jared grabbed them and kissed her fingers, making lavish noises. Vanessa laughed. He said he liked her hands, called them lily-white and dainty.

'You're sweet', she said.

'Hopefully she'll get your hair too', he said, lifting a handful of her brown hair to his nose and breathing in its shampoo smell.

'She? Do you think it will be a girl?'

'I hope so. A little girl, as beautiful as you'.

'I thought men always wanted boys'. She stroked his cheek. 'A son to grow up just like their daddy'.

'No. Cristina's hoping for a boy, but I'm hoping for a girl. It's a kind of role reversal thing with us'.

Vanessa turned away from him. He hugged her spine close to his stomach and snuggled his face into her neck. She stared at the wall.

The bus crosses over into the outer rim of County Kildare, leaving behind Dublin and Vanessa's well-known territory. It crawls over an s-shaped bridge and into the village where Jared and Cristina live. Vanessa stands, the plum of her belly sitting high; she pings the bell and steps carefully down the stairs. Once on the street, she asks for directions to Captain's Hill; a woman tells her that it is on the other side of the road. She walks haltingly up the steep hill, her pregnancy bulk slowing her down. Stopping to rest on a roadside bench, she lets the thoughts she has been pushing down leak through.

I'm allowed to change my mind – it's my body, my life. My baby. And he loves me. Yes, he does. And I love him too. Cristina won't mind: the baby isn't even hers anyway. It's mine and Jared's. Ours. She can adopt a baby, plenty of people do that. And I'm giving back the money, every last cent, so she'll have that. She'll be glad of it. Cristina can go to Asia and buy a baby – they're all doing it. It probably won't be a boy – they're hard to get – but that will be grand; she won't mind.

The baby trammels her insides: Vanessa places her hands over her stomach, following its movements, and wonders if the small hard lump she feels moving across her skin is a tiny hand or foot. The baby is very active now: jumping and careening around. She laughs.

'Your daddy loves me', she says to the mound of her belly.

It's best to let Cristina know, she thinks, rising from the bench and continuing up the hill towards their house. The sooner it's all out in the open, the better. She'll understand. It's over between Cristina and Jared now; he doesn't want her anymore. Cristina won't be upset, she'll find someone else. Some other man. Some other baby. Not mine. She's not having what's mine.

ABOUT THE AUTHOR

Nuala Ní Chonchúir was born in Dublin in 1970 and lives in County Galway. Her poetry was first anthologised as *Molly's Daughter* in the first Arlen House *¡DIVAS! New Irish Women's Writing* collection in 2003. Her debut poetry collection, *Tattoo ¦ Tatú* (2007) was shortlisted for the Strong Award. Her short fiction collections, *The Wind Across the Grass* (2004) and *To the World of Men, Welcome* (2005), were published by Arlen House, and in 2005 she edited the second *¡DIVAS! New Irish Women's Writing* anthology, 'A Sense of Place'. Her third short fiction collection, *Nude*, will be published by Salt in the UK in September 2009. Nuala has won many short fiction prizes, including the inaugural Cúirt New Writing Prize, RTÉ's Francis MacManus Award, the inaugural Jonathan Swift Award and the Cecil Day Lewis Award. See: www.nualanichonchuir.com

BIBLIOGRAPHY

Molly's Daughter anthologised in *¡DIVAS! New Irish Women's Writing* (Arlen House, 2003), poetry.

The Wind Across the Grass (Arlen House, 2004/2009), short fiction.

To the World of Men, Welcome (Arlen House, 2005), short fiction.

Tattoo ¦ Tatú (Arlen House, 2007), poetry.

Nude (Salt Publishing, September 2009), short fiction.

AS EDITOR/CO-EDITOR

¡DIVAS! New Irish Women's Writing, 'A Sense of Place' (Arlen House, 2005).

New Writing from the West series, featuring authors Geraldine Mills, Colette Nic Aodha and Órfhlaith Foyle (Arlen House, 2005).

Best of Irish Poetry 2009 (Munster Literature Centre, 2008).

Southword, Nos 14–5 (Munster Literature Centre, 2008–9).

Horizon Review (Salt Publishing, 2009).

AS TRANSLATOR

Cathal Ó Searcaigh, *Dánta Grá ¦ Love Poems*, illustrated by Pauline Bewick (Arlen House, 2009).